BOUGHT BY THE ZANDIANS

ALIEN WARRIOR REVERSE HAREM ROMANCE

RENEE ROSE
REBEL WEST

CONTENTS

AURELIA MINOR 2, SLAVE AUCTION

NAKED, strapped to a post on the auction block, I suck the blood from my cracked lower lip.

Please let this be quick.

The longer I stand up here, trembling and on full display, the greater the chance of some being searching my barcode and discovering I'm wanted.

I guarantee my former master, Akron, put a bounty on my head the moment he realized I escaped. And he doesn't even know the secret I'm keeping. The one that would spell my death.

Yeah.

So it was escape or die. And I escaped. Briefly.

Three Ocretions walk by, chortling to themselves. One of them slaps my tit and the three roar with laughter. I make my stare blank, like no sentient being is inside my body, as I fiercely pray they won't stop. Ocretions would know to check my slave barcode and trace my history back to Akron. It wouldn't take them more than half a planet rotation to find out about the bounty and deliver me to my rightful owner.

I hold my breath until they move on.

Apart from them, I really don't care who buys me. I plan to escape again as soon as possible. Supposedly, there's a planet where human slaves can go and be free: Jesel. It's wildly dangerous, but that doesn't bother me. My life is probably forfeit, anyway.

I wriggle in my tight straps. The animal hide bites into my skin. My arms and legs have gone numb, but worst of all, the one around my neck is too tight and I can scarcely breathe. I work to slow my inhalations because panic will only make it worse.

The market is full of beings of every species. Most appear too poor to even offer twenty steins for me.

Of course, I don't look like much. I'm filthy and bruised, covered in scrapes from getting here. When I first arrived, I rubbed some of the crimson dirt from this planet on my hair to cover the exotic color. Blondes are considered a rarity amongst human slaves. Unfortunately, I was caught moments later. At least I was grabbed by a small-minded, greedy smuggler, whose only interest was a quick sale.

Two large purple beings with horns stroll idly along the stalls of the market. Muscles bulge beneath their clean white tunics and they carry old-fashioned swords on their belts.

Real Zandian warriors.

I've never seen one before, but I've heard of them. They study for battle until it becomes an art. Long rumored to be extinct, the recent word around the galaxy is they just took back their planet with a tiny army.

They look at me from across the crimson dirt expanse and one of them leans into the other one and says something. When they start walking in my direction, my heart inexplicably hammers.

I moisten my cracked lips with my tongue. I can't decide if my response means I'm afraid or excited.

Afraid. Definitely afraid. Warriors like these are probably bounty hunters. They're after the price on my head.

And that may be true, but as they come closer, tingles run across my skin. Must be the damn breeding hormones. I'm never excited by males.

But maybe I just hadn't met the right species before. Because when they stop in front of me, my nipples tighten, and my breath shortens. Apparently purple aliens with horns are exactly my type.

One of them inhales deeply, his nostrils flaring.

The other one reaches out and slides his thick fingers under the animal hide strap that binds my neck to the post. My eyes fly wide and I try to suck in a breath against the increased constriction. But then he yanks it away from me, tearing it from the post and throwing it to the ground. I drag in a lungful of air and cough.

The Aurelian trader lifts the same gun he used on me and points it at the male's chest. "Get back! You can't set her free."

Neither Zandian moves. They don't flinch at the sight of the gun, nor do they lift their hands in surrender. "Your slave was choking," my liberator says mildly. He has a deep voice that does strange things to my knees. "You should take care with how tight you strap them. No one will buy a dead female."

The trader scoffs and pinches my cheeks, drawing my bleeding lips together. "This one wouldn't die so easily." He shows them the bite mark I left on his arm. "She's a *liineor.*"

I have no idea what a *liineor* is, but I assume it's some wild beast from this planet.

The Zandians don't move, but the upper lip on the leaner one starts to curl. He says something under his breath in their language, and his friend nods. Neither of them take their gazes from me.

At first glance, I thought their eyes were brown, but now I see they're purple, like their skin. Or have they grown *more* violet? The leaner one takes a long, slow perusal of my body. "How much?" He sounds only half interested, but that could be part of the bargaining game.

I can't decide if I *want* their interest. I shouldn't. These males are dangerous. Very dangerous. They're trained to kill, and they appear highly intelligent.

So I should be hoping they mosey away and find some other vendor to hassle.

But instead I find myself praying they buy me. For no reason other than because I can't stand the thought of them walking away.

The larger one lifts my tangled hair from my shoulders and peers at my neck. His fingers brush my bare shoulder. He's so close I smell the scent of his skin—

masculine and clean. He drops the locks back in place and says something to his friend in Zandian.

Fuck.

They *are* smart. He just saw my real hair color but he's playing it cool.

"Where did you get her?" he asks. He has a square, hairless jaw and a cleft chin that probably makes every female in the galaxy drool when he goes by.

The trader lifts his chin. "It doesn't matter where."

"So you don't have her file? She's not legally yours?" the leaner one asks.

Oh fuck. They're asking way too many questions. The next thing you know, they'll be checking my barcode. I twist my neck to the side and lean forward, catching the "V" of skin showing above the Zandian's tunic with my tongue. I flick once. Twice.

He catches me by the hair and pulls my head back, gazing down at me with amusement.

"I think she likes you," his friend observes with a chuckle.

He holds my hair in a fist too tight, but I don't think he means to hurt me. He's just too strong, or unaware of how much weaker my species is. He leans down and brushes his lips across mine. At the same time, his free hand cups my mons.

I jerk, more from surprise than anything. And because every other time a male has grabbed me there has been unpleasant.

But it isn't this time. He rubs the pad of his finger lightly through my folds and I'm stunned at how wet I am.

His horns stiffen and lean in my direction while he

watches my face, his nose almost touching mine, amethyst eyes burning.

I pant, heat curling like smoke through my belly.

"One hundred fifty stein," he says. He removes his finger from my pussy. I'm itchy and hot. Needy for his touch to return.

"Three hundred," the vendor counters.

"One seventy-five. Final offer." He releases my hair and takes a step back.

"Two fifty."

His friend scoffs. He shrugs and walks away.

The fucking vendor lets them go. Three steps away. Four. Five. "Two hundred," he calls to their backs.

They stop but don't turn. They seem to be in conversation with each other.

"One ninety." The vendor tries again.

It takes the broad one two long strides to return. His friend pulls out a burlap bag full of coins while he digs his fingers under the strap around my chest. He rips it off, as if thick animal hide is easy to snap.

I wince as the blood rushes down my arms like a million insect stings. He rips off the strap around my thighs and I crumple, unable to hold myself up. In a flash, I'm swooped up over a broad shoulder.

The Zandian claps a large hand down on my ass. "Come on, little slave. We know just the place for humans who like to escape their masters."

CHAPTER 2

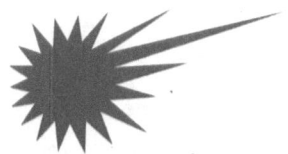

 *enn*

GORDE CARRIES the human over his shoulder to our ship, drawing a few curious looks from the intergalactic traders who choke the market. I knew the second we saw her Gorde was going to want her. Who wouldn't?

She's incredibly beautiful, even with the ridiculous mud-job she did to disguise her hair. It's pale blonde—the color of moonlight, which makes her exceedingly valuable. Humans have interbred so long there are few humans with anything but brown color hair. Red-haired and blonde human females sell for at least three times as much. So do particularly dark-skinned or light-skinned females—any unusual trait sells for more.

Her eyes, too, are a striking color. Pale blue-green. The color of the crystal lakes on Zandia. The ones I've only seen on old holos.

Soon, we'll be back home. We were hoping to find a Zandian female to mate, as unlikely as that may be.

Gorde and I were sent to search for any remaining Zandians scattered throughout the galaxy. King Zander wishes to extend a personal invitation for all to return. The demands of repopulation require we have as many in the gene pool as possible.

Somewhere along the line, Gorde and I got it in our heads we might be lucky enough to find one last female of our own species. Tomis and Erick were fortunate enough. Why not us?

But I know that gleam in Gorde's eye. He's already thinking the human is ours.

Which is too bad, because we could sell her for a huge profit. Maybe I can still talk him into it.

After we've had our way with her, of course.

Because there's no way either of us will last a planet rotation in the same ship as this enticing female without needing to claim her.

And considering the condition we found her in, it's easy to ignore my guilt at using her as a sex slave. Surely this has been her use for all of her adult existence.

We'll treat her well, and resell her to a decent being. No harm will come to her. And Gorde and I certainly know our way around the human female anatomy enough to please her. We'll have her screaming for release before we leave Aurelian airspace, I guarantee it.

Gorde voice activates the hatch and carries her onboard our craft—a shiny new fightership provided by King Zander for our special mission.

"Let's get our little slave cleaned up," Gorde says, but

walks past the washtube. I realize when he reaches the back hatch, he intends to use the open wash area normally used to hosing down dirty equipment.

Ah. He wants to wash her himself. Or rather, he's inviting me to join him in washing her. There's no way the three of us would've fit in the washtube.

I trail after them, admiring the lovely human's form. In her upside down position, the pale roots of her hair are even more obvious.

Gorde sets her upright on the metal surface and I watch her face. I don't catch any sign of resentment, nor do I see the simple slave's expression of devotion or seduction.

This human carries only wary alertness. She's not overly afraid, nor does she appear particularly trusting.

If I were to bet, I'd put Zandian crystal on her being very smart for her species.

I wonder how she ended up on the auction block in Aurelia.

I'm sure if I scanned her barcode, I'd find out she escaped her former master. There could even be a bounty out for her return.

Even as I consider it, something in me rejects the idea. And not just because Gorde seems taken by her. No, I'm not in a hurry to get rid of this enchanting creature too soon, myself.

The prospect of enjoying her thoroughly has me far too excited.

Gorde turns on the spray hose and strips off his clothes. I shuck mine as well.

The little human's face remains impassive as she scans

our naked bodies, but her lips part and her nipples harden the way they did when Gorde touched her in the market.

We still haven't spoken a single word to the slave herself, but we speak in Ocretion so she can understand us. It's a subtle power play—one Gorde and I have used a hundred times in all kinds of situations, from bargaining for goods to fighting for our lives.

I pick up the hose and turn the nozzle until the spray fans out lightly. Gorde maneuvers her until she's standing right in front of me. "All right. Let's wash the stench of the market off her."

I start with her head, rinsing the mud from her hair. It runs in red rivulets down her tantalizing body. She blinks the water from her eyes and shoves her hair back from her face, but otherwise makes no protest.

"It's even prettier than we suspected," Gorde says, picking up a strand of her moon-pale hair. With the mud washed out, it lies in a smooth sheet down her back.

I step in closer and bring the spray to her neck, then shoulders. When I get to her breasts, I let my free hand wander over them, testing their size and weight.

"Mmm. Firm breasts. Perfect size to fill my hand," I observe.

"Let me try." Gorde steps up behind her and wraps both his hands around her breasts from behind. "Yes, you're right." He squeezes her nipples.

She shifts from one foot to the other, but still offers no protest.

Good little slave. Well-trained.

Gorde releases her to find a skin cleanser and returns. "She's quite dirty," he observes with a casual air as he rubs a dollop of cleanser between his two palms. "It will probably take some time to make sure we get every crack and crevice clean."

My cock, already thick, shoots out even straighter. It's only just beginning to hit me how lucky we are. We just scored a beautiful, valuable human slave. One who appears perfectly willing to allow us to do anything we like with her.

My conscience pricks a bit. King Zander doesn't allow humans to be kept as slaves on Zandia. While humans must prove themselves willing to participate in the rebuilding of our planet, and be sponsored by a Zandian, they do retain a measure of free will on our planet.

By withholding that bit of information, we're coercing the beautiful slave.

Then again, judging by the scent of her arousal, she's not entirely opposed to our actions.

We can always explain her new situation later. After we've used her.

And played with her.

And delivered light punishment for running away from her former master.

And that thought has me groaning, stepping close to our slave so her peaked nipples brush my chest. I hold the water nozzle to spray her back as I cup her mons in the front.

She lets out a *puh*—a little exhale that makes my dick so hard I'm sure it would break off if she grabbed it. She's juicy wet, her pussy swollen and open like a flower. Ready for tasting. Ready for claiming.

~

Danica

OH STARS. It must be my changing hormones. I've never been so receptive to any male before.

Of course, my well-being used to depend on making myself fully available to my master, Akron, but I mean truly *receptive*. As in—I'm dying for their touch, ready for whatever they wish to do with me.

I don't even know their names, although *Master* always seems to suit in a situation like this. The one right in front of me looms—a mass of solid muscle, his purple-hued skin hairless and smooth. His horns tilt toward me, like they're erogenous appendages. The other —the one who threw me over his shoulder—stands behind me. He's even bigger than his friend, his interest as obvious. His cock brushes my hip as he lathers me with cleanser, taking his time, leaving no part of me untouched.

The warrior with the water hose slips one finger into me. I'm shocked to feel how incredibly wet I am for him. His finger is thick, but it's not too much. In fact, it's not nearly enough. I squirm over his finger to take him deeper. He adds a second finger.

I let out a moan and the water hose falls to the floor. The Zandian uses a finger under my chin to lift my face to his and then his mouth descends. I'm surprised by the kiss. I know it's a human gesture of affection, often used during sex, but my former masters have never used my mouth for anything but their cocks.

He dominates my mouth, tasting me, twisting his lips over mine with demand. I part my lips, surrender as his fingers continue to press in and out of me.

The warrior behind me grabs a handful of my wet hair and wraps it up in his fist. He doesn't pull, but my head is immobilized for his friend's kiss now. There's no escaping it.

At the same time, he slides a finger down the crack of my ass and circles my back hole.

I mewl into the mouth of the first warrior. He breaks the kiss and stares down at me. I swear I see amusement mingled with lust in his eyes. "Her pussy is juicy sweet. How's her ass?"

I tense, attempting to squeeze my cheeks together, but it only earns me a sharp slap on one cheek. My mouth falls open and my gaze darts to the warrior in front of me to determine if I've angered them.

"Oh, *veck*, do that again. She makes the sweetest expression imaginable."

My face grows warm. I'm not sure the last time I blushed, but it certainly hasn't happened in my adult life.

The warrior behind me strikes my other buttock. My pussy clenches around the first Zandian's fingers.

"Oh, she loves it." He sounds excited. He pumps his fingers in me, his digits hitting some extra sensitive place deep inside me.

I cry out, my hands flying out to catch his meaty forearms.

The warrior behind me works a thick finger in my ass and I'm completely at their mercy. I try not to move, though my hips want to shimmy and wriggle. Whether I'd

13

be shifting away from the sensations or toward them, I'm not sure.

I pant as they fill me, each of them pumping at his own rhythm, killing me with the overload of sensation.

"Please," I start to whimper. "I need—" I don't finish because my brain's too scrambled to put words together.

The warrior in front of me loops one of my arms around his neck. "You just hang on and keep making those soft, sweet sounds, and we'll let you come, little female."

Holding his neck gives me the stability I require. I press my breasts against his ribs, open and close my lips over his wet skin as my feet dance beneath me.

He pumps faster, harder.

The warrior behind me adds a second finger and I sob.

The males suddenly synchronize their thrusts and I'm filled and emptied at the same rhythm. It gives me the focus I need for my climax to build. My mouth is open somewhere over his pec, and without realizing it, I start sucking hard.

He curses and doubles his speed. My knees buckle. A strangled sound leaves my throat and then I hurtle into my climax. My muscles spasm around his fingers, and my anus attempts to close around the finger in my backside.

I scream into his chest as the waves of release buck through me. Only when it's passed and I'm hanging limply from his neck do I realize I've sunk my nails into his skin.

They ease their fingers from me and I nearly collapse. The warrior in front reaches around to extricate himself from my grip, and the one behind scoops me into his arms.

"Let's bring her to the sleep chamber to examine her," he says.

This whole time they've spoken more about me than to me. But I suppose I am more of an object than a being to them. As a slave, I'm used to such treatment. Taking offense would get me nowhere. What's odd is that I find their discussion about me somewhat pleasing. Almost arousing.

Maybe it's the appreciative way they discuss me. They're enjoying me, or rather, enjoying my body, and apparently my body enjoys them quite a bit, too.

I'm not sure I've ever experienced the pleasure I just found with them, embarrassing though it may have been.

They carry me to a small chamber in the ship where a raised platform takes up half the room. The big warrior lays me on my back on the platform and they both loom at the edge, studying me.

I'm shocked to see I marked the slightly smaller warrior when I sucked his chest. I've never done such a thing, and I fear he'll be angry when he sees it. He notices my gaze and looks down.

"You must've pleased her, Benn, if she left her mark on you," the bigger one says, chuckling as he strolls to open a cabinet on the wall.

The one he called Benn reaches a hand behind his neck and rubs where I hung onto him. When he brings his fingers away, they're marked with a tinge of purple blood.

"Forgive me, Master," I say quickly. "I did not mean to use my nails on you."

He offers a wicked grin. "I don't mind it, little female, but perhaps we should punish you, just the same."

I stiffen, pushing up to my forearms.

The bigger one returns carrying a bottle of some kind of liquid. "Oh, certainly," he agrees. "She loved having that ass of hers smacked. Let's oil her up, first. That will increase the sting."

Increase the sting?

I can't decide if I should be afraid or aroused. Do they mean for me to experience pain or pleasure? It's unclear.

Benn holds out his palm and his friend pours some of the oil into it, then takes some himself. Suddenly, two pairs of large hands are on me, pushing me back, rubbing my skin.

It's pure pleasure. I haven't been touched this way—ever. One strokes and rubs oil into my arms, caresses my neck and shoulders, my breasts, while the other works up from my toes, rubbing the aromatic oil into my calves and thighs. He coats my pussy with it, spreading me wide, working it into my outer lips, around my clit.

"Feel how she trembles?" Benn asks.

I start to whine and moan again as the sensations become intense.

"Roll over, little slave. Let's see that ass."

I obey and they spread my legs wide, working oil over the backs of my thighs, my ass, my back.

Smack.

Gulp. The two of them take turns spanking me, one hand falling, then another in quick succession. It hurts—no pleasure at all, just hard, stingy slaps.

I squeeze my ass cheeks together and push up on my

hands, arching my back. I know better than to move out of position—I've been trained too well for that. "Ow! I'm sorry, Masters. I'm sorry! Forgive me."

As abruptly as it started, it stops. The bigger one rubs and kneads my stinging ass as Benn leans over and grasps my hair to turn my face to his. "You're forgiven, beautiful slave," he murmurs and attacks my mouth again, dragging hungry lips over mine in a claiming kiss. "Are you ready to take my cock in that hot little mouth of yours?" His voice is deep and rough, eyes glowing pure amethyst.

I nod quickly and attempt to scramble up, but he rolls me to my back.

"I think Gorde wants to fuck that tight pussy, so I'm going to climb over you and you're going to suck my cock while you spread your legs for Gorde. Understand?"

I swallow. Fuck. Lying on my back to give oral isn't the safest position. It would be easy for him to shove his cock down my throat and choke me without even meaning to. But what choice do I have?

The one he called Gorde pulls my burning ass to the edge of the platform and pushes my knees up. As he lines his cock up with my entrance, Benn climbs over and straddles my head.

My fear must've shown on my face, because Benn stops and simply fists his cock, tugging it as he watches my face. "Don't be afraid, little slave. Tell me your name."

"Danica." If I were smart, I would've thought of a false name to give them. When they first bought me, I had a whole narrative crafted in my head to feed them, but they didn't ask and now my brain's in a different place.

"Danica." He studies me another moment, slowly

stroking his cock. Though I've been naked since the moment they met me, this is the first time I feel bare. If I was unsure before whether they only thought of me as an object, I know now it's not true. It was a game they were playing to keep me off balance. This one actually sees everything.

Behind him, Gorde rubs the head of his cock over my entrance. I can feel the oil he has applied to his length as he eases in. He's huge, but there's so much oil and I'm so turned on, it doesn't hurt or stretch me too much.

Benn doesn't move to jump in the game. He's still trying to decipher me. "Surely you've sucked a cock before?"

Gorde withdraws and shoves in deeper.

I lick my lips, trying to arrange my expression into something agreeable. "Yes, Master."

Another thick, delicious thrust from Gorde. I arch on the platform.

Benn idly toys with one breast, strumming my nipple with his thumb. "Then what are you afraid of?"

I've spun lies my entire lifetime. Whatever my master wants to hear. But for some reason, the truth comes flying from my lips. "Please don't choke me with it."

His expression clears. "Ah." He picks up my fingers and closes them around the base of his cock. "You control it, love. Don't be scared."

I exhale, relief and confidence flooding in to replace my fear. Gorde finds my clit with a finger or thumb and I nearly come unglued, jacking my hips up, my belly shuddering on a breath.

"*Now*, Danica." Benn loses his patience.

18

It's just as well, because I'm suddenly dying to suck his cock. Between the incredible sensations below my waist and his consideration with me, I'm eager to show my gratitude. I grip hard and lift my head to take as much of his cock into my mouth as I can. As promised, he stays in place, letting me move my head and mouth around him. I twist and turn my head, sucking hard, rolling my tongue on the underside. I pull back and rub my lips over the head of his cock, lick a long line up the underside.

Benn's thighs shake, his horns seem to grow even stiffer. "That's it, beautiful," he murmurs.

Gorde grips my thighs and pulls me over his cock in quick pulses, making my mouth bob over Benn's member. I look up to see if he minds, but he's smiling. I squeeze my hand around the base of his cock and use it to pump along his length as I suck him off.

"Good girl," he purrs. "Such a sweet slave."

"Best. Pussy. I've ever. Had," Gorde grunts, slamming hard into me with each word. He thrusts deep, roars and comes, filling my channel with his hot essence.

I suck hard, faster, but Benn shakes his head and pulls out of my mouth. He shifts to lie beside me, and lifts my head to help me lean over him.

Gorde sees what's happening and assists, pulling out and lifting my hips to arrange me on my knees over Benn. He slaps my ass.

"You keep sucking, little slave. I'll provide the motivation."

Another slap.

"Her skin picks up the handprints so beautifully,

doesn't it?" Benn asks as I take his cock all the way down my throat. He grabs the back of my head and curses.

Gorde slaps my ass. It hurts, but excites me, too. That initial spanking shocked me with the intensity, but now that my butt is already warm, already used to their slaps, I almost welcome the pain. Especially with my pussy still throbbing from my previous orgasm and recent fucking.

I use every skill I've learned to please Benn, and he responds, eyes rolling back in his head, broken groans coming from his mouth. All the while, Gorde punishes me with slow, steady slaps.

"Open your knees," he commands, prying my thighs wider. As soon as I'm where he wants me, he slaps between my legs, his fingers connecting with my clit, palm punishing my labia.

I come off Benn's cock and shriek. Gorde slaps me there again, harder. "I didn't say you could stop sucking."

I resume my job, frantic now, although I'm not sure if I'm frantic to avoid the punishment or because I need to come. The pulsing in my swollen clit has reached epic proportions, heat and desire coiling up in my core.

Benn roars and comes, hot streams of his essence shooting down the back of my throat.

At the same time, Gorde starts spanking my pussy with light, quick slaps. I moan around Benn's cock, sucking him in long strokes that move my whole body.

The need to climax is so great, I'm blinded. I do some-thing I've never, ever dared do with another master—I reach my hand between my legs to touch myself. Gorde covers my fingers with his, helping me push over my greedy flesh while at the same time, he spanks my ass with hard, swift strokes.

I come, screaming around Benn's cock, thrashing my head until he uses my hair to lift my mouth off his spent length.

My eyes must've been wide with shock at what I'd just experienced, because Benn chuckles and pulls me down on top of him, embracing me. It's such a foreign position. Never, in any of my experiences, have I been held in a being's arms following sex. It's wonderful.

Transcendent, even.

And if I were smart, I would get a handle on all these feelings and wrap them up tight. Because I have a plan. And it doesn't involve me remaining a sex slave.

Even if it is to two very attentive and hot warriors.

CHAPTER 3

 *orde*

I'M IN LOVE.

I know Benn was holding out hope of finding a Zandian female, but this human is perfect. Granted, we haven't said more than a few words to each other, but getting to know her will be an utter pleasure.

How could it not be when she's such a beautiful, compliant little slave?

And yes, I know, she's not really our slave as our King doesn't allow slaves. And we'll tell her that...soon.

Really.

But in the meantime, I'm loving the *veck* out of dominating her, especially when she's so willing and responsive.

I watch Benn hold her for a moment, then crawl up

and join them. I'm not jealous of Benn. The two of us have been best friends since we were kids. Sharing is something that comes naturally. But it looks too sweet to pass up. I want to know what her soft, lush form feels like draped over my body, too.

I lie on my side, propped up on an elbow, and rub her ass. It's still red with my handprints. I hope to *veck* I didn't spank her too hard. She definitely didn't seem to mind it, but if I leave actual marks on her, I'm going to feel terrible. I know humans are a weaker species—they experience more pain and don't heal as fast as Zandians. Perhaps that's why she was so worried about making Benn bleed when she scored him with her nails.

"Are you all right, little slave?" I push her almost dry blonde locks from her face. "Danica?"

"Yes, Master," she murmurs. Her lips are swollen from Benn's kisses and now I do feel a stab of jealousy, or maybe it's just the need to claim. I lean forward and take her mouth, working my tongue between her lips as Benn did.

She responds, ever sweet, parting her lips and allowing me to take whatever I desire.

Somewhere, some little voice tells me it's too good to be true, but I push the thought away. Benn will tell me himself soon. He'll probably argue that we sell her because she'll fetch a good price, but I'll refuse.

We're keeping her. Or I'll keep her if Benn won't see reason. Zandians require females. If not our own species, then we need human females to breed.

A thought strikes me and I break the kiss. Most sex slaves are sterilized to prevent unwanted reproduction.

What if she can't breed? Would I still want her? *Veck*, yes. Although eventually we'd need to find a breeder, too.

"Danica, little runaway slave." I run my hand up her back. "Where did you come from?"

Her body, which had been languid from the sex, stiffens.

"Aw, don't ask her that, Gorde. If she lies, we'll have to punish her, and I was just enjoying how soft and sweet she feels against my skin."

I tug her down between us so we can sandwich her in. "Right." I fix her with a stern look. "We won't accept lies."

"No, Master." The answer is automatic, but I see intelligence behind her eyes. King Zander and the others who have taken human brides have already proven how greatly underestimated humans are by the rest of the galaxy.

While they may not be as physically strong and their psyches have suffered from generations of slavery, they have untapped intelligence and talent.

"Have you been sterilized, little human?" I lift her hair from her neck to taste her skin.

She stiffens again. "No, Master." Her voice sounds choked. "My contraceptive hormones were recently discontinued."

I push up to lean on my hand instead of elbow. "So you're capable of breeding?"

Her gaze is wary, but she gives a single nod.

I throw a triumphant glance Benn's way, but he appears as wary as our slave.

"Humans make good breeders for our species," I remind him.

He sits up and scoots off the sleeping platform, as if

physical distance from me and the slave will save him from discussing this with me. "I'm well aware," he says mildly.

I want to knock his teeth out, but to appease him, I say, "It doesn't mean we can't keep looking for a Zandian." Immediately, I wish I hadn't spoken in front of Danica. Or had used Zandian, which few in the galaxy understand.

She's gone wooden.

"No offense to you, at all," I say. "I'm certain you'd make an excellent breeder for us."

Her nostrils flare, but she says nothing.

Benn gives voice to what she's probably thinking. "She didn't ask to be our breeder."

This is where I should tell her she's not obligated to breed with either one of us.

I notice Benn's not in a hurry to tell her, either.

Both of us are first class bastards.

CHAPTER 4

My comm hums and flashes, awakening me. The human —Danica—sleeps, her lashes fluttering against her cheeks. I see her pulse in her neck, the way her chest rises and falls. Is she dreaming, the way we Zandians do?

The comm flashes again, so I get up, my mind switching fast into military mode. "Captain." I stride away from the sleeping platform so I don't wake her.

Captain Rok's face flashes in front of me. "I need you and Gorde to divert to Hectan-3. There's a potential Zandian there."

I lean forward. "Female?" My heart pounds with a mixture of excitement and concern. I glance back at Danica. Yesterday, finding a female Zandian for myself was the only thing I wanted in the universe. Today—

He raises a hand, gives a short bark of laughter. "Male.

If you leave now, you can be there in under an hour. Take shield precautions; there are Ocretion ships in the area. Talk to Raxx for on-planet advice."

"Understood. Send me the exact coordinates." I hesitate and my face feels hot. "Ah, we—acquired a female." I clear my throat. "A human."

Now he's the one who steps forward, raises his voice. "Where?" A muscle tigthens in his jaw. "Safely?"

"Aurelia Minor. Her owner—former owner," I correct, "wasn't aware of her value." Something twists in my chest at the thought of her pretty eyes, the way they widened in fear at the auction, and I shake my head. "Believe me, we know how to keep a low profile."

He presses his lips together. "We can't delay on the rescue mission. Taking her with you—will it be a problem?"

"No. We can handle this. We can always sell her off if she gets difficult." I cross my arms, trying to ignore the tiny stab of guilt in my chest. Of course, I'd make sure to find an owner who would treat her well, and not hurt her—

"Do what you need to, but get our Zandian home. Top priority."

"Understood." I end the transmission and gesture, excitement leaking into my voice. "Gorde." He's by the flight console, studying a digimap with glowing points.

"Orders? Where to?" He can always read my tone and body language. He flips his fingers and the map of places where we've found Zandians dissolves, showing our current location in the universe. "Who is it?"

"A male." I don't need to explain what kind—it's the only kind we're after.

He curses under his breath and stands up, eyes on me. "Captured or free?"

I shrug, check my comm for info. "Unclear. But there's a prison there, so it doesn't look good."

He grimaces. "Not the perfect time." He tilts his head to the sleep area. "But we'll figure it out. She should be all right, yes? She doesn't seem...overly traumatized." The fond look on his face makes me roll my eyes.

We both fall silent for a few seconds. "She doesn't," I agree. "Although I have little experience with humans." I don't bring up the possibility of selling her, or getting rid of her to make our mission easier. It's not because I'm second guessing it. It's just that Gorde will go orbital if I do, and I need him focused.

"You mean no experience," Gorde snorts. "Apart from talking once or twice to King Zander's mate."

I roll my eyes. "Like you're any better?"

"She loved my experience last planet rotation." He chuckles.

"She tolerated yours. It was mine that drove her crazy." I punch his shoulder.

He laughs, then turns back to the map, where a soft ping highlights a flashing blue light. "That's their loc?"

I nod. "What do you know about Hectan-3?" I glance over at Danica—still asleep, although now she's shifted, and has one long, graceful arm over her head, covering her eyes. I smile and feel arousal grow, remembering those arms, and her gorgeous legs, wrapped around me.

If a human feels so good, I can't even imagine how amazing it could be with an actual Zandian female. Although it's interesting, because Zandian females, the few I've seen, don't appear to have those luscious breasts and curvy hips—

"It's not back there, I know that much." Gorde's voice interrupts my reverie. "Basic way station. Refueling for most common craft. Uninhabited, except for vendors, and miners—it can't sustain civilization, but has lots of tin deposits. And the prison." He raises his eyebrows, reading from the comm device. "Recently bought by the Ocretions from the Ta'ab for a sum not made public, but reputed to be 1.2 billion stein."

I whistle. "Stars. Why do they want a prison on a barren outpost?"

He shrugs. "Smuggling would be my guess. In addition to acquiring prisoners and collecting bounty."

"What is our Zandian doing there?" Unease makes me stand tense and clench my fists.

"Probably stuck in the prison. We'll find out soon."

"When we arrive, she'll need to stay on the craft." My blood boils at the thought of our vulnerable slave in the hands of the Ocretions. Not that she's ours. And I still want a Zandian female. But I'm no monster. *Veck*, after one night of enjoying her body, watching her eyes light up with passion and pleasure, there's no way I'm letting any other being hurt her.

"Without a doubt." Gorde frowns. "Can we trust her?"

I shrug. "She needs a compelling reason to stay." I frown, part of me wishing she'd stay simply because she wanted to. Because she wanted us. Just because it would make things easier, of course.

Gorde crosses his arms. "It's best if she thinks, at least for a while longer…that she's our slave."

"Agreed. It's the best way to keep her safe."

He nods, his face taut. "I think…"

Whatever he was about to say is cut off as our human appears behind him, smelling of our mixed essences, an aroma that is as *vecking* enticing as anything I've ever experienced.

She blinks up at us, her long pale hair tousled around her perfect face, and I want to grab a handful of that silky heaven and tug her to my mouth, push her down to my cock, which is already straining at my flight pants.

I swallow hard. "Did you sleep?"

Her face grows pink. She blinks and her long lashes, pale like her hair, make me think of soft things. "It's the first time I've ever slept for over six hours in a row, since I was…" her face shutters. "In a long time." She crosses her arms, glances at the two of us. "What now?"

I admire her blunt approach, almost as much as I'm intrigued by her bare toes, her delicate feet, and the way her sleep shirt—a large one of Gorde's—does nothing to hide her luscious form.

I shoot a glance at Gorde. "Right now, you're going to eat. I understand humans require thrice-daily sustenance."

Gorde nods. "The rations in the stock bay should sustain you. In the silver and white containers. I've unlocked them for you."

She swallows. "Thank you. I meant, though"—she waves her hand—"after that. Where—what—are you going to do with me?" She curls up the toes on one foot and I see her clench and unclench the long muscle at the front of her thigh.

"Whatever we want." My voice comes out harsher than I intended, and she tenses, shrinking back a few inches. I amend it with, "You're ours now, and you'll do what we say. Here and on Zandia."

"Yes, Master," she answers immediately, as if by rote. But now she's clenching her fingers together. Then she puts one hand briefly over her belly, and I wonder if we were too rough with her last night. I hope we didn't *veck* her too hard. Is she sore?

Gorde adds, his voice smooth, "And as long as you're obedient, you have nothing to fear from us. Understand?" He reaches out and tips up her chin with one long finger, his eyes trained on hers.

She breathes out, a shaky little sound and nods, wordless, her pretty head bobbing. The way it bobbed when she was sucking my cock.

I force myself to concentrate. "There will be no reason for us to give you a real punishment, or do anything… more drastic, as long as you obey us. Tell me yes."

Her voice is low and cracks. "Of course, Master."

She's scared but trying to hide it. It's wrong, but my cock stirs to life again.

I turn away to mask my arousal. "I need to check the flight path. We're going to stop at a planet and you're going to stay onboard the craft while we pursue business."

"Yes, Master." This time her voice is more fluent, and she leans forward, eyes alert. "Ah…which planet?" She blinks rapidly.

"There's no need for you to know that." My voice is

harsh again, but I don't want her to have that info. "It's hostile, inhospitable, especially for your species. That's all you need to know."

"I see." She bites her lip.

"Then go eat something." I gesture. "It should be self-explanatory, easy to find the rations in that pod. And... clean yourself. If you want." How often do humans bathe? I know next to nothing about their species.

Gorde touches her arm. "Don't be afraid," he encourages. "As long as you're loyal to us..." he raises a brow. I hold back a smirk. He's the master of passive aggressive threats. Not something I ever thought I'd see him use on our female. I mean, *the human.*

I turn back to the console as she walks to the supply area, forcing myself not to make more eye contact. When she's out of earshot, I turn to my partner. "Updated tracking shows his location inside the prison."

"*Veck.*" He blows out a breath. "This will be tricky."

"That's a max security unit. With just the two of us..." I keep an eye on Danica to make sure she's not eavesdropping. Far across the craft, she tentatively opens a silver and white container, glances at me as if unsure. I nod to her and smile. She puts a hand to her mouth, drops it, smiles at me, then takes out a silver packet and examines it.

He wrinkles his nose. "How do you want to play it?"

Danica's got her brow pursed and I wonder if she had any idea what kind of food she's looking at.

"Can she read?"

"What?" Gorde frowns.

"Danica. I know most ag slaves can't, but I don't know about sex slaves."

"I have no idea. Probably depends on who she served before us." He gives me an irritable head shake. "What's our entry plan for the planet?"

I see her rip the packet and take a small piece of the dried fruit inside. She tilts her head, takes another bite. I breathe out. "Bounty hunters looking for an escaped convict?"

"Could work. Returning property to its rightful owner." Gorde nods. "Everyone respects that."

Across the room, I see Danica stiffen. It was almost as if she is able to hear Gorde's words. My belief that she's a runaway is no longer the only suspicion I have about this human.

No, we're not returning you, little slave.

I keep my eyes on her as I speak. "The prison will be hectic if they're transitioning ownership to the Ocretions. We can play that to our advantage."

He taps his wrist and contacts our operations specialist back on Zandia. "Raxx. If I needed to get into an Ocretion prison on Hectan-3 as a bounty hunter, what would I need?"

Danica

THEY THINK I can't hear them, but I'm listening intently as I eat the dessicated apples and prunes, the walnuts.

Human food to match my body, things that originated on a long-dead planet.

"Thank Mother Earth," I whisper, touching my belly. I need the sustenance now more than ever, and my appetite seems endless as I finish one packet, then another.

I sneak glances at them. Both are strong, tall, well-muscled, and handsome. I've seen my share of males from around the universe, and these two appeal to me on a visceral level.

But I can't stay with them. They want a breeder, someone to carry on their own genes. Oh, they may not mind mixing their DNA with those of a typical human, but what I carry inside me is something they could never accept. Not all of me.

The taller one, Gorde, approaches me, and his dark purple eyes search me, starting a slow burn in my body. "Danica." I sense a gentleness from him under the rough exterior, something sweet. I'm drawn to him with an impossible pull. How can I like him this much, so fast?

"Thank you." I hold up the empty packet in my hand. "It was delicious." I find it hard to look away from his eyes. A tingle starts in my core. Mother Earth, again? My body is ready for him.

His shoulders loosen. "Good. I was worried it wouldn't...suit you." He holds out both hands. "I'm not familiar with what humans eat."

"Even though you have human slaves on your planet?"

He swallows and a tendon moves in his neck. "I am not currently mated." His voice is stiff. "The Zandians who have human mates are far more knowledgeable about their traits."

Mated.

Interesting choice of words. One generally doesn't mate a slave. Akron certainly never considered me a "mate". I was a sex slave, a servant, a breeder. Never a mate. What kind of society do they have on their newly recaptured planet?

"So you are generally kind slave owners. Moderate." I try to imagine life there.

He tilts his head and looks away from me. "We are not unkind." When he looks back, he smiles. "You will be treated well, Danica."

"But all females are breeders." My stomach clenches. I've had my share of breeding. That's why I'm gunning for freedom.

"So are the males, if you think about it that way."

I tilt my head. "What way?" He seems so earnest, I get lost in his amethyst eyes.

"Our population was greatly diminished. Zandians, all of us who are left, must do everything we can to ensure that our society survives and thrives. We're needed to provide young who can carry forward our genes."

"But you don't want human males. Or any other species, right?"

"No." He shakes his head. "Well, we have some human males—the ones who pledged their fealty and fought by our side to regain our planet. They will forever have a place on Zandia. But we won't accept new male immigrants. We can't have them, Danica. We have few enough females to go around as it is."

"And if one...came to Zandia, somehow? What would happen?" I'm not planning on sticking around to find out, but I guess I should know, in case I don't escape before we arrive.

"Enemies are killed. Neutral beings are sent away, somewhere else."

"Where? I mean, where would you send a human male?" I have to stop the urge to cover my abdomen protectively.

He blinks. "There's a planet across the galaxy where it's safe for humans. Well, as safe as they can be. Jesel. But they can't stay on Zandia."

Jesel, yes. That's what I'd heard, too. A planet where humans are actually free.

"What about non-humans? Say, a being from the galaxy who may not be your enemy, not specifically, but is known as a violent, cruel species? Would you ever try to rehabilitate them?"

"Why are you asking?" He touches my shoulder. "You will be safe, Danica. We have excellent defenses. Any cruel species are absolutely not welcome, I can promise you that. We will never welcome them to Zandia. We'd drop them in their tracks as soon as we know they're here. No exceptions. Understand?"

"I do." I shiver. I understand I have to get myself to Jesel, because sticking with these males is not a viable option.

Benn comes up. "What are you talking about?" He scowls at Gorde, but when he touches my hand, the tenderness on his face makes me smile. These two warriors, these fierce creatures, both want me.

"I was telling her how she will be safe on Zandia." Gorde touches my other hand, and for a second, I feel like the three of us are a circuit, all connected, in a way that feeds a hunger in my soul. I close my eyes, and grab both of their strong hands, their powerful fingers pressing into my smaller ones. I like how they automatically adjust their touch already to my body, more exposed and fragile than theirs.

But I can't get used to this. Their planet is not for me, and I need to remember that my goal is not to end up as their breeder on an outflung rock at the edge of the galaxy. I need to make it to that planet where the humans go.

~

Gorde

DANICA TAKES a breath and looks up at me. "I'm cold. Are there more clothes I can wear?" She touches the sleep shirt. "Something warmer and more protective?"

"Of course." I move to the side of the craft and use my wrist comm to open a locked cabinet. "Here are spare garments we have on hand. See if anything fits you." I don't know if the trousers and boots will work but they look warm.

Her face breaks out into a huge smile and she gasps, her whole expression lightening. "This is perfect."

While she starts sorting through the things, I tap Benn's shoulder. More of a punch than a touch. "It's time to focus." He's staring at her with a curious expression on his face, like he's trying to figure something out, and we need to get into warrior mode for our planet foray. "Raxx couldn't get into their prison system remotely—it's locked down hard. We're going to need to play mind games with them."

He laughs, immediately focused. "My favorite. *Veck.* You be the asshole, I'll be the calm one."

"Oh, *I'm* the asshole?" I narrow my eyes.

"Call it like I see it." He grins. "Who else punches their partner anyway just to talk?"

"You *vecking* excrement," I curse, scowling.

"Just like that." He nods. "Excellent job, my student." He smirks. "Follow my lead and we'll be fine."

A chime sounds from the control panel, signaling our arrival into Hectan-3 airspace, and both of us turn our heads. I hold my breath, because if our craft isn't accepted by their air control system and cleared to land, we're *vecked* before we even start the op.

But a second later the second chime comes, the one that signals the go-ahead, and I relax.

As the craft begins the usual series of auto-adjustments for descent, I look at Danica. She's holding boots and clothes in her arms, and she looks intent as she watches the panel from across the room.

Too intent.

I nod at Benn, and then at her.

He glances over. "Yeah," he says softly. "What are we going to do about it?"

"I hate to say it but..." I retrieve a pair of cuffs from the side compartment. "She's not going to like this, but I think it's necessary." I hand them to him.

He puts up both hands and raises his brows. "We

already decided you're the asshole, for good reason. So you do it. Get into character, brother." He laughs. "You can make it up to her later with your tongue, I'm sure."

"*Vecking* beast," I mutter at him. But it's a chance to touch her, and I'll take it.

I stride over to Danica. "Give me your hand, slave," I order.

She doesn't resist, not exactly, but she doesn't give her arm easily, so I reach back and slap her ass, hard. My cock surges to life, but there's no time for that now.

"Ouch," she complains, reaching back to rub, but I grab that hand too. It's the work of a few seconds to cuff her delicate wrist in the glowing magnetbands, the ones controlled by my voice. I anchor the left one to the lock in the craft wall.

"I'm sorry," I tell her, and I mean it. I touch her face, but she moves her chin away, and I see her chest heave. "Are you crying?" My voice rises as I try to look at her eyes. It's something humans do, I know, when they feel strong emotions. The thing is that I also feel a whole host of emotions, watching her. The need to protect her. Keep her safe.

No, she's not crying. She's angry.

"You don't need to restrain me." Her voice is high and tight, brave, but her whole body trembles.

"We need you to stay on this craft, Danica. So you can be safe. I don't want..." The idea of anyone else getting their hands on her makes me shudder.

"I plan to. What would I want on an inhospitable planet? I just want to get somewhere safe." There's conviction in her tone. But the way she was looking at us before, so alert, her whole body on notice…

I clear my throat. "I know how to read signs of flight. You'll stay cuffed here until we return."

"What if you don't?"

I harden my voice, because there's no time right now for intimacy. "You better hope we do, because anything out there is going to be a *vecking* lot worse than what we have planned for you."

I grab her chin—not roughly, but firmly, and look into her eyes. "I mean that, Danica. There's nothing for you on this planet."

She nods. "Yes, Master." She still looks angry, but her eyes are moist.

"We will come back. I promise you."

She looks at the floor, where the clothing she selected lies in a heap. "I'm still cold."

Her arm is warm as I touch it. But I remember how she shivered before. I grab a blanket from the container and drape it over her shoulders, my fingers wanting more. "Here. We'll give you time to dress when we return."

Her mouth tightens, and she shrugs. "All right." Her eyes are downcast now, and she slumps against the wall. "Can I at least sit down, or will I have to stand the whole time?"

I adjust the anchor point where her cuff is attached. "It slides. You can stand or sit. You just can't move away from this location." I hesitate. "Are you in pain?"

She makes a sound like a laugh, but there's no humor in her eyes. "That's not a yes or no, Master." She pulls at the cuff.

My voice tightens. "Does your wrist hurt?" I touch her skin just above the cuff. "Is this too tight?"

"My wrist doesn't hurt." Her voice is flat. "I'll be fine."

"So will we."

She looks up at me, and I'm surprised at the expression on her face. "Come back safely." Her voice is almost fierce.

"We plan to. Always do."

CHAPTER 5

We're already in character as we exit our craft. We dressed in the typical garb of bounty hunters—rugged clothing in neutral colors, lots of pockets for gear, some body armor. Platinum armored boots. Cuffs at our waist. Horns and skin disguised with headgear, so nobody knows we're Zandian. Walking tall, cocky, because we *vecking* own the world. As if we've been in a thousand fist fights, and we're ready for a thousand more. Like we welcome brawls, leaning forward into violence and danger.

"A lot of ships here." Gorde glances around us as we step into our ground craft, which we undocked from our main vessel.

"It's a popular station. On the flight path for a planet cluster. Ugly."

He scoffs. "These places are always bleak."

The landing area extends as far as the eye can see to the left and right, and there are over a hundred craft docked here: Transport ships, bulky, bloated with precious cargo, flash to the left, most of them with armed guards on duty on and off craft. Diplomatic vessels with the insignia of the galactic sign for neutrality—which is not always honored—are in a section to the right. The sleazy transport craft, the ones that typically dupe their passengers and steal their money, unless you're tough as *veck* and have the physique to kill without a weapon.

And then the rest of us, crafts of various sizes and shapes, each with our own plans and destinations, litter the ground in even rows. The refueling pods rumble back and forth, lights flashing.

"Stinks." I wrinkle my nose and look at the rusty sky, thick with particulates and smog.

"It's the mining. They don't care if they wreck this planet."

"Use it up and discard it." I frown. Ruining things for profit hurts in my core. After all, it's what the Finn did to Zandia—or almost did. Thank *veck* we have our planet back.

"Right to the prison, then?"

"Yeah. Bounty hunters don't waste time. And we need to work fast. We changed our ship ID to that of a bounty craft, but I don't know how long that will fool them if they dig."

I set the coordinates, and within a tick, we see the foreboding walls of the penitentiary building towering above us, gray, steel, thick. Impenetrable. Walking to the entrance, we smell rotting garbage mixed with the emissions from the local mining ops.

Gorde grunts. "Raxx said they disconnected the electro fence while they switch ownership."

"Good. They're not as organized at they want to seem." I scan the foreground, senses alert. I touch the bag of stein at my waist. "And Ocretions are always open to bribes."

"Here we go." I take a breath. "Ready?"

"I was born ready." There's that tone in his voice, the one full of eager energy.

I raise my hand and the Ocretion guard at the entrance pushes a button. The glass wall slides open.

"Bounty hunters." I snap the words out, staring at the guard. "Understand you have my legal property on this site."

He doesn't react, and then a slow, unctuous smile spreads across his face. "Everything in this place is my property, now. Civilian." He smirks. "You'll address me with my rank, if you want to speak further. General Ofte. You low-lifes never get it right the first time."

I snarl, as if I'm insulted, and lean forward, grabbing his collar. "You fetid corpse. I should cut you up right now."

He stiffens under my hands, but his gaze doesn't waver. He's not worried, which means security here is tight. *Veck.*

"You do that, and you two will end up in the Pit." He laughs. "Not a place anyone wants to be for a day, let alone eternity."

"Refusal to relinquish legally owned bounty is punishable under galactic agreement X-27." I force myself not to react to his threat. I release him with a shake, and dart my eyes to the side. More guards laze in a side room, but they're listening. Watching. Armed. "Something I know you Ocretions take advantage of, often."

"Who's going to enforce that here?" His smirk makes it easy for me to act further enraged.

"Maybe I will, right here and now." I reach forward again, but Benn is there in a flash, his hand on mine.

"Stand down," he snaps, then his voice eases as he looks at the guard. "Heard that pay here is going down with the new ownership."

"What does that have to do with anything?" But the guard leans forward, eyes glittering.

Benn shrugs and leans on the half wall, the partition separating the guard from us. "Doesn't matter much to me. My salary's the same, regardless of what I bring in." He gestures to the locked inner doors, beyond which lie the holding cells. "In fact, I got a bonus this solar cycle for my efforts." He raises a brow. "Nice to be recognized. Handsomely."

"Must be." The guard slides his eyes from Benn to me, to the other Ocretions in the side room. He clears his throat. "Perhaps I could see if your property is here. No promises."

"Compensation is commensurate, of course. With what we get." Benn touches a pouch at his side.

"Indeed." The guard finally steps forward. "But you can't take weapons into the prison, naturally. They'll be safe here." He gestures at a silver safe behind him. "So if you care to relinquish your protection, I can gladly take you on a tour."

We expected this, but it still feels like ice in my chest to hand over my stunner and my dagger. Not that Master Seke didn't train us to use anything and everything as a weapon, including our hands and feet. The guard scans us with a handheld wand, and takes my extra knife from my ankle. "Come, then." He leads up to the main door and uses his fingerprint to open it. "Biometrics makes it easier to prevent escapes." He smirks at us, his eyes cold.

"As it should be." Benn's voice is easy. "Living quarters here are difficult, I suppose. On the planet."

"We get by." The Ocretion lifts his hand and another door opens, thick glass and steel.

"We recently…acquired…a shipment." Benn keeps pace with the guard, while I follow behind. "Luxury items from Matrigar. Worth a hundred thousand stein. As soon as my ship leaves this airspace safely with our prisoner's live bio IDs on board, I can have it diverted here. Automatically in the system, no override. To thank you for your troubles."

The guard laughs. "Careful, aren't you?"

"Is there any other way to be?"

"Show me." The guard stops in front of a cell, a dank, dark hole in the wall that makes me want to shudder. Instead, I roll my eyes and tap my foot.

Benn pulls up his comm. "All we need is both of our digisigs and it's done. Assuming we exit with our appropriate cargo, of course."

"Of course." The guard affixes his thumb to the tablet. Then he raises his hand and the door slides open and lights come on.

I catch my breath. Blinking in the back corner of the

47

cell, dirty and bloody, is a Zandian. My heart fills with anger to see one of my own in such condition, and the red that fills my eyes clouds my vision.

"He was...uncooperative." The guard smirks, goes up to the Zandian, and kicks him in the ribs, evoking a painful sigh. The male's mouth is so battered he can't talk. His eyes are swollen shut. "But we have ways of ensuring that our prisoners go where we tell them." He removes a shock stick from his waist and readies it. "Get up."

I clench my fists, ready to roar, to rip off this guard's head. Benn steps forward. "If he's not in condition to fly, the deal is off. We need him alive."

The guard steps back, puts up his hands. "Of course." He looks at us. "Wanted for theft and smuggling, level H. Carries a death sentence, or so his file reads." He turns to the prisoner. "Happy travels. He's all yours."

Our headgear hides our horns, and the SkinSan masks our color, but the Zandian recognizes us as brothers; I can see it in the way he tilts his head, looking at us through swollen slits, the way he gasps when our hands grasp his arms. I'm enraged that they coded him like a slave.

I want to be gentle, but we're bounty hunters, so I keep my expression and movements impersonal. "Come with us now or it won't end well for you," I snap to him, roughly hoisting him to his feet. "Can you walk?"

He licks his lips and croaks. "I...need..."

He needs crystals, or he'll die. But just being near us is having a restorative effect, because his breathing evens out and he blinks.

'You'll get water on the transport ship," I say, frowning at him, shaking my head. We walk him down the hallway, and my pulse races as we reach the final door, because what I see makes my adrenaline surge.

Two Ocretion guards stand in front of the door, hands on their weapons. Two more stand to the side, one of them talking into a com. They all turn slowly to look at us, as if watching a holo vid. Entertainment. One of them smirks and rubs his hands together.

Our guard stops in front of the door, but doesn't open it. He steps back. "Our journey together ends here." He raises his shock stick and the others draw weapons. "I think that having three Zandians could be a wonderful bargaining chip. More important to me than your steins. I imagine King Zander would give a fair amount of crystals to get you three back, with most of your limbs intact." He eyes the bag at Benn's side. "Although we'll take that, too. I'll miss the luxury items, but oh, well." He laughs. "New facial recognition tech with deep-IR. You can't fool Ocretions. Not anymore." He smirks and lunges, and so do the others.

Benn and I drop the rescued Zandian, and whirl to face our opponents. I leap and kick, using the heel of my boot to smash into the Ocretion's sturdy jaw. The crack of his bone and his high scream echo off the polished corridor walls, and his shock stick flashes as it flies from his hand. Benn grunts as one of the Zandians hits him with the stunner, but his protective garb prevents damage. Still, he stumbles, and I grab him, keeping him on his feet, before turning. "You got this," I mutter, turning to the next guard.

"This is what you can do" —I kick— "with your"—a powerful punch sends one of them flying into the smooth wall, his skull hitting with a satisfying crack, his neck shooting forward and then going slack, his eyes draining of color as he slumps down the wall to the ground, blood trickling from the corner of his mouth— "deep. IR."

I elbow the Ocretion in front of me with all of my force, right into his nasal bone, and feel it give. Benn drops the last one and the two of us pant, Benn bending over, hands on knees. My eye stings and when I wipe, my hand comes away purple with blood. Mine, because it doesn't have the sulphur-like stench of Ocretion blood and innards, although their stink is on us now, all around.

Benn's gaze is wild, his eyes fierce. "We need to get out. Now."

I take a deep breath and grab the fallen Zandian, who's breathing shallowly, his face pale, his horns shriveled. "He's dying. We need to get him to the ship." I hoist him to his feet, ignoring the pain in my left side from the blaster blow.

Benn wipes his mouth and grabs the Zandian's arm. "Let's go."

We're already out of the prison, and our transport is still there in the lot. Nobody pays us much attention; bloody beings dragged off are clearly not out of the norm here. As we get in, I scan the prison behind us. "It's a matter of time before the entire local force of Ocretions comes after us."

"Ocretions love a good hunt." Benn grimaces. "And torture before killing their prey."

I grunt, setting the coordinates for our ship. "Once we get him on board, we take off immediately and get out of this sovereign airspace. You set the pilot details and I'll get him into the med pod."

But when we reach our ship and board, not without difficulty, I curse to myself, because our problems have just magnified. The magnet cuff dangles from the wall, empty. Danica is gone.

Danica

THE BOOTS ARE TOO BIG, but they protect my feet from the baking hot ground. This planet is dry and dusty, and my forehead breaks out in sweat immediately as I leave the craft. I cough, and grab my mouth—I need to be quiet, no matter how fetid and polluted the air. My lungs sting as I breathe, short shallow breaths, and I cough again as I dart from behind our craft to the next one.

"Our" craft—no. My captors' craft.

I push back the memories of our night together, the surprising passion, and scan the area. I won't be safe until I'm a free woman. I'm definitely not going to Zandia to be a breeder, and have my secret found out. No, I'm going to take my chances out here, because in this vast galactic parking lot, I know I can find a craft that's headed to the place I need to go. Jesel.

I pull the thick, hanging jacket closer around me, glad that the clothing bin included headgear, which I used to tie up and hide my hair. With my baggy, rough garments and the dirt I've put onto my face, I can pass for a male.

On this way station, beings of all species intermingle, albeit for a short while, just here to refuel or stock their craft. They're technically no-aggression zones, these outposts, and that weighs in my favor.

I suck air and walk fast to the next craft, hover in the shadows created by the vast wing, peering into the distance. Yes! About 800 yards from me I recognize the logo of the InterTrack passenger shuttle. Other slaves whispered about this being the transport that takes anyone, no questions asked, no need for pesky paperwork.

I straighten my shoulders and stride forward, keeping my head high, my gait strong. When I reach the craft, I nod to the Falladian standing guard at the base of the entry station. "I'm looking for passage."

He stares at me with all three eyes, scratching his head with one tentacled arm. His other arms cross over his chest. "We're full." His gaze slides past me, then back.

I extract a bag of coins from my voluminous jacket. Gold I took from Benn's bag. "I can pay in gold. No taxes, no fees. Just pure stein."

He blinks, his blue eyelids closing like those of the lizards that ran around on my old planet. "Full is full."

"Double." I shake some coins into my gloved hand.

When he doesn't react, I raise my eyelids. "With a bonus for you."

He doesn't move for a long time, and bile rises in my throat. Every sound behind me is like a shot to my gut. Are they coming after me yet?

Then he blinks again, that slow open and shut. "Triple. And only as far as Tellurex. I don't want to know your final destination. You can get another transport there."

"Done." I resist the urge to glance over my shoulder. A re-fueler pod zooms past, making sloshing and clanking sounds, like some gears are worn, and disappears around a craft further down the tarmac. I see various beings around, and my unease grows—I need to get out of sight, fast.

"Weapons will be checked and stored for the duration of the flight. To ensure the safety of all passengers." His long, thin mouth curves up into a grin, revealing long, razor sharp, whisper thin talons, in tapered rows of three, on both upper and lower jaws.

"Of course." I tense my thighs, clench my fist. Resist the urge to shudder.

"We depart in one hour. You can board now—"

He breaks off, stepping backwards, his eyes widening. I whirl around, heart in my throat, and panic when I look right into the flat-featured, ugly face of a squat Ocretion.

"What do we have here?" the Ocretion asks, eyes glittering as he examines me, his gaze far too sharp for my liking.

The Falladian shrugs. "Transport passenger. Who's asking?"

"Prison Specialist X23-G." The Zandian flashes a badge. "Looking for runaway slaves." He raises a sleek flashing device. "Surely you don't mind if I do a quick scan, just to ensure your passengers are all legal?"

The Falladian stiffens, and his eyes redden. "This is a neutral way station, guard. I don't care who you are, my passengers are off limits." His body starts to swell and expand before my eyes, his muscles puffing out into hard ridges. An acrid sweaty odor fills the air. He glances at my pouch of gold. I know he only cares about my money, but I'm grateful for his resistance to the Ocretion.

The Oc doesn't move at this display. "It won't take but a second." He grins, an oily nasty smile that leaves his eyes flat and cold. "As we Ocretions now own the local prison, we have additional rights to look for escapees on the planet."

I suck in air and cough, the acrid fumes burning my lungs. There's probably not enough oxygen here for me, and I feel dizzy and cold, hot, sick. But something in my gut twists, something hidden and mysterious, telling me I need to react —

I sense it before it happens; the Ocretion reaches out, serpent fast, his clawed nails flashing in the lights from the trans craft, and I've already leapt aside. Anticipating. I guess my reflexes are still working.

"Mother Earth!" I whirl and run, coins flying from my fingers like sunbeams, falling to the parched ground. Adrenaline gives me speed, and I fly, racing around obstacles with ease, my mind moving fast to plan my route.

But he's faster. It's only seconds before I feel his hands on my jacket, and the breath is wrenched from me as he stops me in my path, whirling me around roughly to face him. We're back at the transport craft, and I could weep— my salvation so close, yet so infinitely far.

"You're a human," he spits at me, his foul breath making me gag.

"I'm not. Take your hands off me," I snap, struggling in vain.

"If you're not, then what's that on your neck?" He leers at me. "The first digits signify human."

Mother Earth. My headgear has come loose, exposing my barcode. I grab the scarf and rewrap it. "None of your concern." I need to get onto that trans ship—once I'm on, he can't board. Nobody can, unless invited by the craft owner.

"You're done." He laughs. "Your life is mine. Don't fight it, or I'll make this far, far worse." His ugly sneer brings bile to my throat.

I take a deep breath and turn to run again, but he grabs my arm, pressing in hard with his repulsive hand, and I scream now, with all my might, although there's nobody here who cares. Not even the Tellurian—he wants easy money; he won't get involved in a spat with an Ocretion. No sane being would.

My head spins with terror, and then, to my utter surprise and relief, there's Gorde. Strong, panting, anger and concern in his eyes. "Let go." With one vicious punch, he drops the Ocretion, and I'm pretty sure I hear cracking bone as the monster falls to the ground, his hand loosening on my arm like a hideous flower blooming open. I know he's dead before I see the dark maroon spread of his blood.

"Danica. We need to get the *veck* out of here, now!" He grabs me, but I'm not capable of moving.

Frozen, I stare. "I…"

"What are you *vecking* thinking?" he roars into my face. "You're coming to Zandia with us. You have no right to wander around this *vecking* desolate shit-hole of a monstrosity full of violent creatures whose lives are worth less than nothing. " He spits at the Ocretion on the ground.

I have no love for Ocretions. But his words remind me why I needed so desperately to get onto that transport shuttle.

"Let me go!" I scream, tugging, scratching at his hands with my nails. "I need to go. Let me go."

"Go where?" His breath mingles with mine, both of us panting. His face is an inch away. "With this creature?" he gestures back at the transport ship, to the Tellurian, who's hovering in the shadows, still inflated, watching. "Who will probably murder you or sell you back to a slave auction the *vecking* second you depart this planet?" His eyes are fierce and wild. "You're defenseless, Danica. You can't run around like this. You'll be killed in a heartbeat." Even in my panic, I notice that his face is tired. And that purple blood trickles from a wound on his temple.

His grip tightens. "And you belong to me, now. To me and Benn. Let's go. *Veck*."

He starts to walk, and when I resist, he simply grabs me and tosses me over his shoulder, like I weigh nothing.

"You don't understand." I slump over his shoulder, all of my strength gone, my muscles quivering. "I can't go with you. Please."

He doesn't respond, but quickens his pace until he's jogging. My head pounds from the jostling and the stress, and by the time he reaches the craft, my skull is splitting.

He dumps me unceremoniously back by the wall and attaches the cuff.

"Let's go," he snaps, and Benn immediately sets the craft into motion. The departure is faster and rougher than any I've experienced, and although the AirPulse keeps me safely in place during the sharp ascent, I suck in my breath, dizzy, as we escape orbit.

"Are we clear?" Benn's voice is taut.

"Yeah. I dropped the Ocretion who identified her as a human when I found her." Gorde gestures at me. "No one followed us, either, and by now we're far enough away that they can't, even if they try."

"So we're not going to get any surprise visits to Zandia," drawls Benn. "Looking for missing property. That's a relief."

I hear gentle beeps from the side area, and see that the med pod appears to be occupied. Although I crane my neck, I can't see who—or what—is in the pod. I shudder as the craft leaps forward, anxiety and relief mixing with nausea.

"Another breeder for you?" I snap. "I hope she fought back. I wish she'd given you a worse injury." I scowl. "Also, you both smell terrible." I put my free hand over my mouth, as a new wave of dizziness rolls through me.

Neither Zandian responds.

"I need fluids." I suck in a breath. "I don't feel good." I blink, the scene in front of me blurring and softening into a watery landscape. My cuff doesn't move with me this time, and when I slump down, my whole arm goes taut as I hang forward and gag, my shoulder twisting.

"Help her," snaps Benn. "I've got this."

Gorde is at my side in a flash with a flask of clear liquid. "Here." He adjusts me so my arm isn't being strained and fixes the cuff so it can slide. He sits down, cradling me in his lap, and holds the tube to my mouth. "Drink it."

I gulp all the sweet juice and wipe my eyes. "The air on that planet…"

"Is harsh. We told you." His voice is hard, but I hear something else in his tone, and his eyes scan my face. "*Veck*. You could have ruined your lungs if you were there longer. It's not for humans, Danica." He reaches up and rubs my face. "You're crying."

"No, I'm not." I look away. Damn. It must be the hormones. I never cry.

"Why did you run?" He taps my chin, and his tone sharpens. "We told you to stay. How did you get out of the cuffs?"

I shrug.

"Tell me." His hands tighten.

"Ow." I pull back, and he loosens his grip immediately. "I don't know how, Gorde."

"Don't lie to me." He scowls at me. "You've got one punishment coming already for your escape. Don't double it."

My stomach flutters. "I'm telling the truth. I just…" I blink.

"You just what?"

"I looked at the cuff and I wanted it to release. And it did." I bite my lip.

"That doesn't make sense. Do you have some magnetic implant I don't know about?" He grabs my free hand, turns it over to examine the underside of my wrist. We both look at my pale, unmarked skin.

"Not that I know of." I shudder.

He narrows his eyes. "So you did it with mind-control. Really, Danica?"

My eyes fill with more ridiculous tears. "It must have malfunctioned." I shake my head. "Lucky for me."

"No. Not lucky at all," he snaps, then softens his voice. "Where did you think you were going?"

"To the only place humans can live free." I look across the room to the med bay, where the pod flashes soft red lights.

He scoffs. "You'd never make it there a quarter of the way, alive. It's impossible, Danica. Even we have trouble getting there undiscovered. Don't you know how..." he breaks off. "Do you realize how fortunate you are that we found you before you got on that transport ship?"

"I didn't know. I thought if I could get onto that ship..." I touch my stomach. "It was instinct. I'm tired of being a slave."

He looks away and his body clenches under mine. "Too bad, Danica. And disobeying us will only make it worse for you, so I suggest you obey in the future."

"So you're going to punish me?" I look up at him. His features excite me, even at this moment when all I should feel is fear. Maybe it's the way he's holding me against his chest, so firm. Maybe it's the way he released me when I said ow. Or perhaps it's the look of concern in his eyes. Most likely adrenaline from the escape.

He leans in until his lips are nearly brushing mine. His voice is low, and his eyes flash. "Yes. We are. You're not going to like it, either."

"What if I just said I was sorry?" I can't look away from his gaze.

"Oh, you'll apologize."

"I will?" I breathe out the words.

His hands soften on my arms, and he circles my wrists with his strong fingers, holding gently. "Repeatedly. You'll beg for mercy over my lap, Danica."

I blink. Over his lap doesn't sound too frightening. Besides, his face burns with passion, not anger.

"And after that?"

"After I spank you? Then Benn will take a turn." He smiles. "Until we're both fully…satisfied that you've been thoroughly and sufficiently disciplined."

I shiver, but it's as much from arousal as anything else.

He runs a finger down my cheek. "Don't worry. You'll learn your lesson well enough." He gives me a wicked smile. "And we're going to *vecking* enjoy every second of teaching it to you."

My traitorous body thrums with desire. I don't know why his threats arouse me.

"Perhaps there's a better way to teach me the lesson," I suggest, my voice low. Our lips are practically touching.

He smirks. "No, a spanking is usually the very best thing." Then his lips brush mine, so softly it's like air. But before I can kiss him back, the med pod beeps in a new pattern, louder, aggressive.

He jumps into action, sliding me from his lap, getting to his feet.

"Check it," orders Benn, but Gorde's already striding over.

He leans over the pod. "He's fighting the Replenish."

"Then it's set too high. Adjust it."

"Already done." Gorde types rapidly on the pod

controls, and the beeping goes back to the previous pattern.

"Who's in there?" I lean over, still cuffed to the wall. "You said he? It's a male? Why do you want a male slave?"

Neither of them answer, and I tug at the cuff. "Can you let me go, please?"

Benn leaves the console and joins Gorde; the two of them peer at the pod, then talk in a low voice. I tilt my head until I can hear. It's a gift; all I need to do is turn my ear in the right direction and I can catch the softest sounds, if I really focus. I only noticed that I could do it since…I frown, unease filling me.

"He's stronger. Look at his horns. They're normal again. And the blood transfusion worked."

"When will he regain consciousness?"

"Let's telecom with Dr. Daneth. We need his advice on what to do next. Thank *veck* he created this med pod for our rescue missions."

"Or else he would have died." Benn gestures at the pod.

I sigh and lean against the wall. Then I look at the cuff and focus. *Release. Let me go.*

Nothing happens, so I try again, focusing harder, but only manage to make my head hurt.

I glance again at the Zandians. What did happen before? Maybe the cuff malfunctioned right when I wanted to leave…the other options really don't make sense. Especially since I can't replicate it.

Benn comes over and sees me pulling at the restraint. "I'm going to release you to clean up, wash, eat. You can't overpower us, so don't try."

"I won't." I hesitate. "I'm sorry."

"Are you?" He gives me an even look.

I duck my head, thinking of how best to answer, but he just shakes his head, leaving me alone.

After I'm clean, have used the medikit and dressed in a flowing dress—apparently they no longer trust me with boots and camo gear, even though we're in the middle of space—I sit quietly in the module chair while Benn and Gorde talk. They glance over at me from time to time, and although I can hear them clearly, I can't understand now that they're speaking in Zandian. I speak Ocretion, one of the most common trade tongues in the galaxy, and the language my master uses. *Former* master. I shudder.

From across the craft, the two Zandians notice. Gorde scowls and snaps something, and Benn shakes his head. "Are you all right?" he calls, out, then approaches me. His brow wrinkles. "Are you still feeling ill?"

"No. That passed. Thank you." I glance at the pod.

"Your lungs are all right? Your breathing?"

I nod. "The inhaler worked. I'm fine, now. Just a little shaky from the whole experience, I guess." I look again at the pod.

He follows my gaze. "A rescue." He crosses his arms. "Since you clearly won't stop asking until we tell you." I think I see the slightest hint of a smile.

"Not a slave?" I bite my lip.

"No." His expression darkens and he looks away. "A Zandian. Don't go over there. Don't touch the pod."

"Why not?"

"Because I said so." He scowls. "Safety. His and yours."

"Fine." I put up my hands. "I have experience dressing wounds. That's all."

"You do?" He narrows his eyes and tilts his head.

A cold shudder goes through me, as memories rush my mind: Akron lashing out with his claw-like nails, full of rage, but controlled. Always controlled. Slicing where it won't show. Inner thighs. Belly. Leaving me to think about my transgressions, and to clean my own blood, tape up the thin, deep wounds correctly. Taking me to the medic to laser away the scars, only so he could have a fresh canvas.

I put my hands on my legs and take a deep breath. "That one on your forehead. You need to wash it and apply ointment. If you hold it together and affix the wound tape, you can line it up to make the scar thin, nearly unnoticeable." But when I look closely, I see that although the dried purplish blood is still there, mixed with dirt, the wound itself looks smaller.

"Are you healing that fast?" I'm amazed. I reach out to touch his head and he lets me. "Still, you should wash it to avoid infection. Especially if it's sealing rapidly."

"We have more med kits." He points. "I'll use it later. I'm fine."

"Use it now." When he raises his eyebrows, I lift my chin. "Master. Please. I can help."

A beat goes by, while he looks at me. "All right." The corners of his mouth turn up. "Do it." He looks at me, then his jawbone flushes with a deeper purple. "I'll get the kit."

When he comes back, I'm surprised to see that there are vials of unknown medicines and lotions, things not available from the inter-galac trade. Akron always got top of the line everything, that's one thing I can say about him.

"This is specialized?" I hold up a tube of clear gel.

"Created by a human, actually." He smiles. "On Zandia. It helps Zandian skin heal many times faster than it would naturally."

"A human slave? They get to do such work?" I take a sterile wipe and the water tube; dab his forehead. He doesn't wince, but a muscle clenches in his jaw.

"We told you, life on Zandia won't be bad." His voice is even as I cleanse.

When I rub the salve onto the wound, I can see the thin, purple line start to recede, like water evaporating. "This is amazing."

He nods. "Thank you." His voice is softer, as I clear up the debris.

"It's nothing. I've tended far worse."

"Are you a medic?"

"No." I toss the trash into the incinerator bin and close the kit. "Please, I don't wish to talk about my past. Master." I sneak a glance at him out of the corner of my eye.

"All right, but eventually you'll tell us everything," he says, and I can't tell if it's a promise, a threat, or both.

CHAPTER 6

G orde

OUR RESCUED Zandian is still unconscious in the pod, the glow of the healing crystal softly illuminating his lined face. His vitals are stable, and I assume he'll wake by the time we arrive home.

Thank *veck* we got out of that prison. That I was able to find Danica in time to escape. The thought of leaving her alone there makes me feel ill. The more I think about it, the angrier I get. How could she be so irresponsible and disobedient? Before, I was running high on adrenaline and relief. Now, I'm pissed. I'm practically fuming.

Both Benn and I took some time to wash and dress in new clothing. It was a relief to clean off the fetid blood of the Ocretions, which had mixed with my own blood and sweat into a foul paste. But it was talking to Danica that made me feel most replenished.

Danica. I look at Benn and clear my throat.

He nods. "She can handle it now. It's time."

The two of us approach and stand over her. I put my hands on my hips and Benn crosses his arms. She looks up, and her neutral expression turns to one of trepidation. Her hands still on the med kit she was organizing.

"I—" she begins, eyes widening.

"Are about to get your well-deserved punishment," I finish. "Now that we're in safe air space and our rescue is stable, we can dedicate the proper amount of time we need."

Her face goes to the resolute, absent expression she wore when we first saw her on the auction block, and everything in me screams to bring her back to the present, to us. I no longer care about punishing; I want to make her *feel*. Feel us. Know us. Make a connection. And yes, I'm still aching to flip up that gauzy skirt and turn her soft ass pink. But her punishment won't be some impersonal beating, or some shock stick or confinement. I don't know how she's been punished in the past, but it will be different with us.

It will be an intimate reckoning.

I reach down with my hand and affix her with my gaze. "Come, Danica."

There. The intelligence returns to her eyes. I'm not forcing her up, I'm asking for her compliance with her punishment. She hesitates, then takes my hand, her small one warm and delicate in mine. I easily pull her to her feet and in a second I'm seated on the hoverdisk with her across my lap.

Benn sits beside me. "Slide her over," he suggests. "I'll hold her down while you spank her. I'm sure she'll try to get away before you even get properly started."

Danica makes a small sound of dismay, and stiffens.

"Excellent idea." I adjust her so that she lays across both of our laps. "I imagine we should start on her bare ass."

"Of course. Disobedient slaves don't get the luxury of a warm-up through their clothing," Benn agrees. "It's a better lesson if it stings from the start."

"Please. I'm sorry, Masters." Danica twists to look up at us. "You don't need to." I get the sense it's what she's learned to say when she's in trouble.

"So you're sorry you almost got all three—four—of us, killed?" My anger rises up again.

She nods and then sort of sinks down onto my thighs, her body limp, her head to the side. All I can see is that glorious pale hair, all soft and flowing, smelling fresh after her wash.

I swallow. "So it would seem that we do need to, Danica. To remind you who's in charge, and punish you for causing such trouble." Without thinking, I grab a fistful of her hair and tug, forcing her to look at me.

Her eyes are wide, and she seems uncertain, but not terrified. Good. I don't want her petrified—just respectful. She licks her lips and immediately my cock reacts. The desire I feel courses through me, fierce, and I wind my fingers further in her gleaming locks. "Don't you agree?" I continue, but now my voice is lower, and I know she can

67

feel how hard I am under her body by the way she wiggles and gasps.

I let go of her hair and stroke it once. *Veck*, how can it be so soft? Then I pull up her skirt and tug down her panties, reaching over to slide them down her calves and off her body. "Naked, as we discussed. And going forward, all of your punishments will be on the bare. And you'll remember that. Next time we tell you that you're getting a spanking, you're going to remove your panties before getting over my lap, without being asked, or I'll double the spanking. Is that clear?"

"Yes, Master," she whispers.

"Yes, Master, what?" I persist, laying one hand on her soft skin.

She flinches, then relaxes into my touch. I stroke along her buttocks, focusing on the place at the base of her thighs.

"Yes, I'll…if you say you're going to spank, me, I'll take off my panties immediately."

"No matter where we are," I persist. "Or who else is around. All that matters is your obedience."

"Yes, Master," she breathes.

"Why will you take them off?" I bend down to talk closer to her ear. I can see the pulse beating in her neck.

"Because…naughty slaves deserve to be spanked naked," she says, and there's a little catch in her voice. She relaxes her thighs, and I see a glimmer of moisture between them. *Veck*, she's already aroused! Part of me wants to forget all about the punishment and bury myself in her tight pussy. But then I think about how narrowly we escaped, and I strengthen my resolve.

I raise my hand and slap her left ass cheek. Once, again, again. She flinches and makes a small *oh* of surprise, and my cock hardens at the flush of red on her white skin. "Stop," she begs.

"Don't ask me to stop," I warn her. "Because we're going to spank until we feel you've been sufficiently punished."

"If she asks us to stop again," Benn suggests, "we might need to supplement the punishment with a strap or paddle."

"Mmm." I rain a flurry of spanks on her ass. "Excellent idea. She needs to learn to take what she's given, and accept that, as her masters, the two of us control her body. In pleasure and pain both."

Danica sucks in her breath. "That won't be necessary, Masters."

"Then control yourself," suggests Benn.

I spank her other cheek, a little harder, and she wiggles on my lap.

"Ow," she whispers.

"Oh, love, you're going to dance on my lap before I'm done," I promise, and start spanking faster, each slap leaving a ruddy mark on her soft skin.

Before long, she's shifting and making little whimpers, but I'm pleased that she doesn't ask us to stop. I know she wants to; this must sting quite a bit, and her ass is turning the most gorgeous shade of deep pink. Almost red. Her resolve fascinates me.

But what intrigues me even more is her growing arousal. I take a break to let her catch her breath, because she's twisting and tugging and panting on my lap.

Without meaning to, I slide my fingers between her thighs and she opens them wider for me. *Veck*, she's wet. Our little human likes this! I groan, driving two fingers deep into her tight passage. Her warm, wet body nearly undoes me. All I can think about is tossing her onto the covers and starting with my tongue, tasting that honey before *vecking* her hard and fast. But she needs to learn her lesson first.

"Your turn," I snap to Benn. "I've warmed her up. Now you can start the official punishment."

Benn and I both know well that this was far more than a warm-up...but Danica won't. And it might do her some good to worry—make her respect our authority.

"Glad to take over," Benn says smoothly, and we flip Danica so she faces the other way, her hips now across Benn's lap. "She's a delightful shade of red, Gorde. Nicely done."

I wind both of my hands into her hair. "Punish her well. Make her sorry she ran away and disobeyed."

She arches across our bodies, making a breathy sound.

"Of course." Benn slaps her hard, across both cheeks, and she moans, the sound one more of pleasure than pain.

I slide her over and stand up abruptly. "I'll watch." I cross my arms, my cock straining against my trousers. Danica turns her head, lips parted, eyes wild. She glances at me and as our eyes meet, something sparks between us, fierce and bold.

"I'll make sure to provide a good show." Benn spanks her again, deliberately, again. Again.

"Please." Her voice is hoarse with need. "Masters."

"Remember, you don't get to ask us to stop." Benn slaps her again, right on the sit spots. Hard.

She yelps but presses her hips down into his lap, and moves her thighs restless. "I'm...I want..."

"What do you want, little human?" He spanks again.

"Please." She whispers, shutting her eyes. Her hands are in fists. Her ass is a glorious red, hot and mottled with our marks, and the scent of her arousal is even stronger than before.

~

Danica

THE SPANKING STINGS, but like the first time they punished me, it also turns me on. I hope they're going to make love to me again, and soon, because my ass can't take too much more.

"Benn," I plead, afraid to ask him to stop, because they sounded serious about doubling the punishment.

"It's supposed to hurt," he says, his voice low. "And we're not done. I think to really make sure you don't forget this lesson for a few days, we need to give you a few strokes with the cane."

A frisson of fear travels along my spine and I stiffen. "The cane?"

"Gorde?" Benn pauses to stroke my hot skin. "Bring it, please?"

"My pleasure." Gorde's voice is hard. I hear him open a

storage locker, and it's less than a few moments before he returns.

He stands so I can see him, and my eyes widen at the thin, whippy implement in his hands. It looks...serious. Long, about as thick as my pinky finger, and polished.

I try to get up, but Benn holds me firmly across his lap. "No," he admonishes.

I definitely don't want the cane. I shiver.

"I'm sorry. I really am." Panicked, I pull at Benn's arms again. "You're going to injure me if you use that." My heart pounds and I panic.

He gives a short laugh and squeezes my buttock. "I promise we will not. Oh, it will hurt. Leave you striped for a few days. But Dr. Daneth—the royal physician—has determined that a good hard caning causes no permanent damage to naughty humans. He even used it on his mate while she was carrying their young. So you can certainly entertain five hard strokes, Danica."

I still. "He did?" I suck in a breath. Then I relax.

"How shall we position her?" Benn rubs his hand over my skin, in small circles. Although I'm sore, it's arousing, and I push up into his hand, craving the touch.

"Have her lean over the sleepdisk," orders Gorde. "Legs nice and wide. If she reaches back or complains, that stroke won't count."

"Good." Benn sets me on my feet. "Did you hear him?"

I bob my head but reach back instinctively.

He grabs my hands. "Did I say you could rub it?"

"You didn't say I couldn't." I don't know where that came from—but I think he likes it, because he growls a little, and his cock—if possible—gets even harder through his trousers.

"You should assume that." He pierces me with his gaze, but softens it with a smile. "Because obedience during a punishment is rewarded. Remember that."

I gulp, mesmerized by his dark eyes. "I will."

"Then do what Gorde told you, and lean over the bed. Nice, wide stance so we can see that pretty pussy while we punish you, too."

I suck in a breath. "I—"

"You're going to obey. If you delay, we'll add strokes. Is that what you want?" He raises an eyebrow.

"No." I bend over the sleeping platform, feeling the fabric soft against my breast. My nipples are hard and the touch of the fabric is arousing. He taps the inside of my foot with his and I spread my legs, feeling the cool air brush my beaded skin. I wish it was his fingers. His tongue. I shift against the structure and moan.

"You naughty little slave," Benn says, humor in his voice. "Look at you, all wet from your spanking. This next part might not feel so good, though." He clears his throat and his tone gets firm. "You're going to stand still for the cane. No reaching back, no kicking, no moving out of position. You do that, you get another one, and we'll keep redoing it until it counts. Gorde and I have all the time in the world to punish your pretty ass, so don't worry about inconveniencing us."

My body surges with adrenaline. "Please." I don't know what I want.

"You want to get started? By all means." He steps over

and takes the cane from Gorde. When he swishes it through the air, standing so I can see clearly, I gasp.

"Hear that?" He does it again. "Sounds like a lot of power. Get ready."

I clench my buttocks.

"No. Relax your muscles." He touches my ass. "Nice and soft for me, Danica. Don't make me wait too long."

I force myself to unclench.

"Good. It's a better punishment this way," he explains, running his fingers over my cheeks. I expect him to start the punishment, but he keeps stroking me, over and over, until I relax into his hands. When he strays close to my cleft, I wiggle, trying to entice him closer. He's almost where I want him, need him. I'm breathing harder now.

"Benn..." I murmur.

"Mmm?" He lowers his fingers.

"Please touch me."

"I am touching you." He's smiling; I can hear it in his voice.

"More."

"Oh, but, baby, you need your caning first," he murmurs, stroking my inner thighs. "And consider your-self lucky"—he touches my sit spots, then the back of my thighs—"that we're only giving you five, and all on your ass. Really naughty humans get a dozen on their ass and another dozen on their thighs, too."

I suck air. "Please."

"Make sure they're good hard ones," encourages Gorde. "I want her to feel this all week when she sits, as a reminder of what she did."

"Consider it done."

Benn touches my back, then runs his fingers up my spine, landing at my neck. He brushes my hair out of the way, his fingers soft, then clears his throat. "Gorde. Hold her down, please, for the first one? She's unaccustomed to the bite and she may need—training—to learn to stay in place."

Gorde puts one strong hand on my neck, the other on my back. His hands are warm and I close my eyes at the touch. Even knowing they're going to cane me, I'm aroused. I want them both. Now.

I hear it before I feel it, the harsh hiss of air. Then I feel impact. And then... "Mother Earth!" I wail and twist, kicking up one heel, trying to get up. The bite is wicked, pure fire across my ass.

Gorde presses his palms to my body, not hurting, but securing me. Not allowing me to leave my position. "Stay still," he admonishes.

"Ouch, ow. It hurts." Tears prick my eyelids and I try to reach back, but he grabs my hands.

"Danica, did I say you could touch?"

"No, Master, but ow. I need to."

"What you need to do"—he strokes my hair—"is to accept this. Benn, she's ready. Go again."

"Of course." I hear a smile in Benn's voice, and then the fire blossoms once again, a new stripe just below the first.

Good thing I'm lying over this sleeping platform, because the pain makes my knees go weak. "It's too much!" I cry out, twisting my hips.

"He didn't even go too hard," says Gorde. "Again."

The cane strikes once, a second time, and now I'm

sniffling and whimpering, shifting my hips.

"Last one," Benn says, his voice surprisingly soft. "You're doing well, Danica. Just one more. Before I give it to you, tell us why we had to cane you, please."

"I-I..." I suck in a breath.

Gorde runs his hands over my ass, making me hiss out my breath. "Ow!"

He slaps my ass once, not too hard, but it stings like crazy on top of the cane strokes. "Danica, we better hear contrition in your tone or I'll take that cane and repeat the punishment." His voice is hard enough that I believe him.

"I'm sorry! I didn't mean to cause danger. I just reacted, all right? It was instinctive. I wanted to get to Jesel. I didn't think about repercussions or how sensible my plan was...or wasn't. It wasn't a logical decision. It was...from the heart." My voice gets low and the tears start to fall.

"All right." Benn steps back. "Last one will be harder than the rest. You're going to thank both of us for the punishment. I don't want to hear anything else but that, or else I will give an extra. Is that clear?"

"Yes." I stifle a sob.

He steps back and the whoosh of the cane is louder than before, and when it hits, I cry out with the instant burn. It's far worse than the others, and I realize how much he was holding back; how much power he has in his arm. But at the same time, need surges through my body, making me wetter than before. I press my thighs together.

I whimper, more from desire than anything at this point, but remember what I'm supposed to do. I manage to get out the words. "Thank you, Master Benn, Master Gorde, for punishing me. I'm sorry!" I clench my pussy muscles. "Please."

"Good." Benn's voice is easy. "Will you try to escape again, Danica?"

"No! Please, it hurts." I twist, trying in vain to reach back again, although if Gorde actually released my hands, I'd go straight for my clit. That's what needs attention right now.

Benn drops the cane; I hear it clatter to the floor. He sits beside me and strokes my shoulder. "Why won't you run?"

"Because it put you in danger. It almost got you killed. I won't do it again." I push my hips up. I hear Benn suck in his breath and smile to myself. They're going to fuck me now, I know it.

"No." Gorde's voice is harsher than ever. "That's not why." He lets go of my neck, and I immediately turn to look at him. Although I can see his arousal in the bulge of his trousers, his voice is taut. "Danica, it's not just us. It's you. Don't you get that? Do you know what that transport worker could have done? You'd have been back at auction in a heartbeat, and probably one in a much fouler, depraved environment. Those shuttle operators are notorious for"—he shakes his head—"unspeakable things. You need to look out for yourself." He takes his other hand off my back.

"That's what I was trying to do!" I struggle to my feet, not even caring that my argument is sort of negating my apology.

"You're never going to get exactly what you want, in

this life," he snaps, clenching a fist. "It's time you grow up and learn to take the best opportunity available. Don't squander what life brings your way, Danica. Us—this?" He waves a hand. "This is the best *vecking* chance you have right now. Don't forget it."

"I'm sorry," I whisper, looking over at Gorde. I can see how badly he wants me—his cock, outlined against his flight pants, is hard and thick. But he's mad at me, more than Benn. And that hurts more than the cane.

Tears come to my eyes at the expression on his face, such disappointment and anger. He sees it; turns away, and that flips a switch inside me, and suddenly I'm sobbing.

Benn responds immediately. "Danica?" He sits me up to peer into my face. He glares at his friend. "Gorde."

"I can't do this right now. You take care of her." Gorde curses under his breath, something in Zandian, and strides away, over to the flight console. He sits down at a chair and I see his shoulders tense, even across the room.

Benn swoops me up into his arms and sits down, putting me onto his lap. "He'll cool down," he whispers into my ear. "Give him time." He licks my neck. "In the meantime I'll help you...recover."

The touch of his lips to my skin is an instant hit of pure desire, and I squirm across his rock-hard thighs, the fabric of his clothing scratchy against my sore ass.

"Hurts?" he murmurs, reaching down. "Lift up." He cups one ass cheek in his hand, and although I whimper at the touch, it becomes soothing in just a few seconds. "I can make you feel better now, Danica." He bites my neck, softly, then again, harder. "You ask for it, I'll deliver."

"What exactly...will you provide?" I close my eyes and lean my head back, exposing my neck. My pulse comes harder.

"Everything," he says simply, and at the tone in his voice, my eyes fly open to examine his face. He's not smiling, not teasing. He looks at me for a long minute, as if he's discovering something for the first time. "Everything," he repeats, and a slow grin spreads across his face. "That makes you cry out in pleasure. You took your punishment like a good girl, Danica. And good girls get rewarded."

"I like rewards," I breathe out.

He moves his hand out from under my buttock and strokes along my thighs. "Open for me," he demands, his voice at once firm and sexy. "I think the caning got you wet, and I intend to find out."

He presses his lips to my ear again. "Although I hardly need to touch to be sure. I could smell your arousal, Danica, and see it while I was punishing you. *Veck*, it was all I could do to finish it."

"Next time, feel free to stop early," I say immediately, then add, "I mean, not next time. There won't be a next time."

"Oh, there won't?" he whispers, resting a finger on my mound. "You sure about that?" He taps my skin, then glides his fingers down to my pussy entrance, pressing into it slowly. "Positive?"

I gasp and push my hips forward, encouraging his exploration. "Mmmm...I don't want to get caned again, ever."

"I don't know if that's quite right." He adds a second

finger and presses them into me, deeper. "Because look at this *vecking* pussy, Danica. A pussy doesn't get this wet unless a pretty little human slave likes what we did."

"I hated it," I murmur, eyes closed again. I can smell his arousal, too, the sweat and need on his body, and it's intoxicating. I open my lips, lick them, wanting him in my mouth—his tongue, his cock. Anything I can get.

"I'm afraid that might be a lie." He adjusts his hand to stroke my clit. "And you know how we deal with that around here, don't you?"

"I'm afraid I don't." His fingers are magical. I'm already approaching the brink of an orgasm, just from his voice, his fingers, his dominance.

"We deal with it"—he suddenly flips me off his lap to the sleepdisk—"any way we like, Danica. Any *vecking* way we want. Is that clear?"

"Yes, Master. Please." I'm on my stomach, and I turn to watch as he strips his clothing, revealing his strong, muscled torso. That long, hard cock, throbbing with need, almost touching his stomach.

"*Veck*, I love hearing you call me *master*," he growls. "Get on your hands and knees, Danica. I'm going to take you from behind, hard. Naughty slaves get *vecked* hard after they're caned, is that clear?"

"Yes, Master." I don't care how he does it, as long as I feel him inside me right now. I'm going to die if I don't get to orgasm soon.

"Your orgasms are mine. Ours. You will never come without permission," he snaps, getting behind me. He strokes my sore ass, and I whimper once, then press into his hands, his touch inflaming me. "Is that understood?"

"Yes, Master Benn." I spread my thighs wider. "Do you understand this?" I look back over my shoulder. "I'd be happy to explain if necessary."

He slaps my ass, not too hard, but a good solid spank. "Don't sass me, human." He grins. "Get back in position and brace with both arms. You'll be glad you did, once I get started." He raises a brow. "And if you're good, I might even let you come."

I moan. "But you said…"

"I sometimes change my mind," he teases. "And as your Master, it's up to my discretion. And, yes, I do understand…this." He runs his fingers along my cleft, all the way from my clit to my anus. "Quite well. You ready for me to show you?"

"Yes, please." I buck my hips, wild for it.

He presses up against me, and I feel his cock, hard as steel, pressing against my ass crack. He reaches under my body to stroke my breasts, pinching my nipples, squeezing. "Do your breasts like this kind of attention?"

"Yes." I squeeze my eyes shut and revel in the sensation. "Yes."

He pumps his body against mine, teasing me with his cock while he plays with my tits. "Good. I'll be sure to remember." His fingers are magical, teasing me until every squeeze, every pinch, gives me a matching ache in my pussy.

"Benn!" I cry out.

"You want this?" He squeezes my tits one last time, then lets go, and finally adjusts his cock so it's at my entrance.

"Please." I wiggle my ass.

81

"Your wish is my command, then." He presses forward. He's thicker than I remember, but I'm so wet it doesn't hurt at all, even when he fully seats himself. When he starts to move, I gasp with pleasure. The first time with the two of them was no fluke. Sex with my Zandians is phenomenal, something I've never known possible.

I don't know why it's so different now, and at this moment, I hardly care. I lose myself in the sensation, fucking him back, pushing with my hips to meet his thrusts, bracing on the bed with both arms.

He grabs my hips and pulls, and I cry out at the feeling.

"You like to be *vecked*?" he growls. "You like my Zandian cock inside you, Danica?"

"Yes!" I can't think. All I can do is move, my motions becoming frantic as my orgasm approaches. "I'm going to come. I want to come."

"You ask permission," he snaps, and slaps my ass hard, once and again.

"Let me come, Master Benn? Let me come," I urge. And although it's more a demand than an invocation, he growls his permission.

"Come, love. Come for me. Right now."

I cry out and let go, allowing myself to tip over the cliff into the most amazing explosion of passion, something that starts in my clit and fills my entire womb, then my entire body. As I lose myself in the waves that come and keep coming, I'm aware that he cries out and comes, too. He stiffens and I feel warmth as he comes inside me. The feeling spurs me into another orgasm, even stronger than the first, and I scream, colors flashing as my entire body is bathed in pure bliss.

CHAPTER 7

WHEN I COME BACK to myself, I'm lying on the sleepdisk. Benn bends over me. "Are you all right?" He kisses my hair, my neck.

"Yes." I stretch, and wince as my ass moves on the fabric.

He frowns and gestures; he's holding a tube of something in his hand. "Roll over so I can put this soothing oil onto your skin. It will take away some of the burn."

"Not all of it?" I oblige, the act of showing my ass to him sparking new desire.

He laughs. "Then what good would the spanking have been? You need some reminder of why you were disciplined, Danica." His hands are strong and gentle on my skin, though, as he massages the slick fluid into my heated ass. It has an immediate effect, soothing the sting until just a warm burn is left. Just enough bite to make me want him again.

"But not too much." He laughs, then bends down to brush a kiss on my neck. "After all, how can we want such a pretty ass to stay sore for too long? Hmmm?"

Tears come to my eyes and to my surprise, a sob breaks out of my throat.

"It's not supposed to hurt." He leans forward. "Does it sting you in some way?" If it's not helping, I can try another lotion—"

"No. It feels good." I clear my throat. "Ak — I mean, I'm not used to having any being take care of me like this." I wipe my eyes. "Thank you."

Gorde speaks up from across the room. "Zandians always take care of what's theirs." His voice is harsh. "Don't forget that. We're not like other species."

Benn's hand stills on my skin. Stiffens. "You're right. We're not." He sighs. "And speaking of what's ours… Danica, we need to tell you something."

I sit up. "What is it?"

He looks across the room, and crosses his arms. "We weren't entirely honest with you before." A tendon jerks in his neck.

"About what?" I blink at him. "Is it about the one you rescued?" I glance over at the med pod, which is blinking one green light and one red now.

"What? No." He looks confused, then shakes his head. He stands up. "It's about…you."

I frown. "I don't understand."

"So, let me explain." Benn takes a deep breath. "What

we didn't tell you before, is that humans on Zandia are not slaves. We don't have the right to take you as a slave."

"Wait...what?" I jump to my feet. My heart pounds and I grab at the silky covering on the sleeping platform, grappling with it, wrapping it around me, awkward. "So this whole time you kept me, I was actually—free?"

"Well, free—not really. Not according to the galactic accords." He steps forward and reaches out to touch my barcode, retracts his hand at my flinch. "But Zandian law is that human females are welcome on our planet, and may stay. But not as slaves. As partners."

"How?" My voice shakes.

"They're sponsored by one or more Zandians, who claim them as mates to bear young. To help rebuild the planet. Human women are perfect partners to mate with Zandians to carry forward our DNA. Both of our DNA." His voices rises with excitement. "We don't have enough Zandian females, so we need humans."

"But what do they...do? Apart from...breeding?" I shudder and wrap my arms around myself as I sink down to sit on the bed.

He tilts his head. "Whatever they want, as long as it supports Zandia. One human is a medic. Another is a—well, she started out with agriculture experience, but now she's one of our top chemists. She works with Dr. Daneth. Another one is a mechanic. Whatever your skills are, we can find something that works." He blinks at me. His eyes, wide and dark, are unreadable. "It's a good life, Danica. You'll be mated with Zandians who match you. You'll have choices back on the planet. And if you accept a

Zandian sponsor and agree to the terms, you will live there safely and we will protect you, forever."

"But"—I can't get past this—"you had no right to take me. Tell me I was your slave." My voice rises. "You prevented me from leaving when you had no right." Of course, I wouldn't have received better treatment from any other being in the galaxy, but it still sticks me.

Benn sits beside me, and after a few seconds, he puts his arm around me. Tentative. A light pressure. "Danica, it wasn't entirely right, what we did. But it was only for your protection. Surely you see how dangerous it would have been for you alone on that planet? Really, there's no way you could make it alive to Jesel, alone. You'd be killed."

His voice is full of conviction, but I don't care. "You don't know that! It was my right to try it, if I wanted. You prevented me. You lied."

"Forgive me for not wanting to watch them cut your *vecking* throat right there," Gorde snaps. "Or drag you off to prison."

I jerk my head—he's in front of me now, eyes blazing. "We just came out of the prison that Ocretion would have used to lock you up. You wouldn't"—he clenches a fist, turns away for a second—"you have no idea. By lying to you, forcing you to stay with us? We saved your life."

I bite my lip. "I don't know what to say." My anger disappears as quickly as it came, and everything seems so clear. I know how Ocretions are. And although the slaves whisper about the passenger shuttle, the truth is that there are also rumors about how dangerous it is.

"Say you forgive us." Benn's voice is low. "Come to Zandia, Danica."

I want to. Mother Earth, how I want to go there with these two males, now that I know what's offered to human women. And since I don't have a route to Jesel, this may be my last and only option.

I touch my abdomen once and a strange sadness twists inside my soul. If they learn about my past, the look on their faces will change from protective passion to anger and disgust. Maybe even murderous rage. But right now, it's my only viable option.

I have to take my chances.

"Yes." I take a deep breath and pretend that everything will be okay. "Yes, I forgive you. Please take me to Zandia."

Benn

WHEN DANICA LOOKS into my eyes and asks me to take her to Zandia, a wave of relief startles me. First of all, I barely know her, and unlike Gorde, I didn't have some kind of immediate mind connection with the little human. Sure, she *vecks* like a dream. But I'm having a hard time giving up my fantasy of finding a Zandian female. I know I'm just feeling a temporary bond with her because of the sex. Dr. Daneth says humans have powerful hormones that can affect Zandian emotions—but I'm not going to be swayed by that. The relief is probably just because I know it's the right thing to do.

I clear my throat. "We'll arrive in a few hours. I'll alert King Zander that..."

A frenzy of chimes from the med pod interrupts, and we all look over as the lid opens with a pneumatic hiss, all the lights flashing green.

"He's awake." Gorde jogs over as our fellow Zandian sits up slowly and winces. He squints as he looks around the pod, his eyes blank, uncomprehending.

"He's still pretty banged up, but the crystal light flood has done a remarkable job healing his bruises and cuts," I mutter. He looks almost whole again.

"Where am I?" His voice, low and resonant, carries across the room. "Who are you?" He frowns, then reaches up to touch his horns. "I was in the prison." He looks at his arms, lifts the left one. "This was broken. I couldn't heal. But it's better." He looks at the med pod. "You have crystals here?"

"Yeah. We rescued you." Gorde nods. "This is Benn. I'm Gorde. We're from Zandia."

The Zandian blinks. "There is no more Zandia." He coughs. His eyes dart around the craft, then back to the crystal, and a strange sensation churns in my gut. There's something off about him, but I can't quite put my finger on it.

"We took it back." Gorde crosses his arms. "It's a sovereign kingdom again. We came to bring you home."

"Home?" The Zandian's voice cracks. He gets out of the pod, one leg first, shaky. The other. He looks around him, turning his head. "This ship. Zandia never had this kind of technology."

"We have a lot of new things." Gorde smiles briefly. "Your name, brother?"

The Zandian blinks. "Well." But he doesn't answer. He looks over at Danica, and his expression twists into something odd and almost fierce.

She sucks in a breath and and steps closer to me. I put my arm on her shoulder.

"Your name." I repeat it, louder, enunciating.

"Taxx." He nods. "But I've been alone and on the run for so long that I go by a different name. And they tagged me." He grimaces, touches his neck. "The med pod didn't remove the laser mark?"

"That can be done on Zandia." I step closer, leaving Danica behind me. "Why were you in that prison?"

He shrugs. "I don't have much memory right now. I've been doing trade here and there, where I can." He glances at the crystal glowing in the med bay. "Random things." He reaches out to run his finger over it. "Do you have any idea how many stein this is worth on the open market?" He raises his eyebrows.

"We do." Gorde's voice is curt. "Every being does. That's why the planet is devastated after the Finn over-mined our crystals."

"I see." Taxx flicks the crystal with his fingernail and it pings, a high perfect note. "I thank you for the rescue." He sits down on the edge of the med pod and reaches up to touch the clear dome that's retracted. "I would have died, there. I thought I was going to die before I'd ever see"—his voice quivers, and he clears his throat—"ah, another Zandian."

"We are honored to bring you home." Gorde's voice

cracks with emotion. "It's a blessing to find another Zandian. The planet will welcome you."

"Who is she?" Taxx looks at Danica. Intent.

"A human female. A rescue. We're taking her to Zandia."

"Is she yours?" Taxx stands up. "I haven't had a female in a long time. Are you willing to share her?" His dark eyes narrow and he steps closer, but the look in his eye isn't one of arousal, but appraisal.

In the past, I would have offered anything and everything to a newly found brother, including my blood. Definitely my new pleasure slave.

But I growl and put my hand onto Danica's arm, just as she makes a squeak.

Gorde snaps, "She's not a toy. Humans are not slaves on Zandia, regardless of what is accepted elsewhere in the galaxy."

Beside me, Danica breaths out a long shaky sigh and her arms tremble. *Veck*, the idea of her being frightened makes me want to stand up and protect her. "She's under our protection on the way to Zandia. Once there, she'll learn the rules from King Zander and….have the choice to select mates." My stomach roils.

"Unless we keep her ourselves," Gorde adds. "As her rescuers, we have first rights." He glares at Taxx.

I don't think that's true at all, and he shouldn't be getting Danica's hopes up, but I hold my tongue. Gorde seems to have gotten over his anger at her, or at least, now that he senses interest from another Zandian, he's clearly eager to stake his claim.

Taxx puts up his hands. "I mean no offense." His eyes linger on Danica a little too long for my liking, though.

I try to shake off the feeling of unease. "You've had an ordeal, and you need to recover," I state. "Rest. If you haven't eaten your weekly meal, we have Zandian and human staples on board. A place to wash. Fresh clothing."

He shakes his head. "All I've had for weeks now is swill. I need sustenance."

Gorde takes him over to the galley and gets him food, shows him the water hose in the back bay. I call in to King Zander to let him know that our Zandian is awake and alert.

Danica touches my arm. "What happened to him?" She's frowning.

"We'll let him eat. There's plenty of time to hear his story."

"Benn?"

"Yes?"

"Thank you." She turns her eyes on me, wide and serious. "For saving me from that auction. For taking me to Zandia. For…keeping me safe."

I look at her for a long minute, into her deep blue eyes, at her perfect lips. Then I force myself to look away. "You're welcome." I clear my throat. "I'm going to go sit with Taxx, get to know him. Why don't you get some rest?"

She nods. "All right. I will."

CHAPTER 8

G *orde*

"WE'RE HERE." The system beeps and the ground system sends acknowledgment. "Zandia."

"May I see it?" Danica scrambles to her feet, eyebrows raised, looking at me.

I point her to the console chair beside mine. "Sit and you can see my screen. Or look out."

"Beautiful," she breathes, eyes wide, leaning forward to peer out the vast curved glass. "Green and blue and purple! I love it." She turns to me. "Does it always glow like that?"

I nod. "The crystals make it so. Can you feel the energy?"

But she's got her head tilted, a curious expression on her face. It's almost like the one she wore during her orgasm, but muted. She sucks in a breath. "I...it's tingly." She touches her face. "Am I supposed to feel like this?"

I frown. "Most humans don't, at least not at first. I don't think." I'm no expert. "Maybe it means you're just more receptive to the crystalline energy."

"That's good...right?" Her gaze is already back on the planet. "I'll really be safe here? It's like a dream. I'm afraid to believe it."

"You will." I want to reassure her, but I'm focused on watching the autosystem as we land.

Benn waits at the other set of controls, in case we need to land manually, and Taxx sits beside him, asking endless questions. By the stars, I think he's talked constantly from Hectan-3 to here, once he was clean and fed. *How does auto-sys work? How does the cloaking system operate? If the ship needs to fire, how do you arm the missiles?* Benn has been more than happy to train him, ad hoc, but something about his interest seems—odd. If I were just rescued, I'd want to know more about Zandia. Maybe just relax in the company of my own kind.

Danica looks at me as our sacred planet looms closer, filling the screen. "Will I be given to—mates—right away?"

My cheeks get warm. "It's customary to first acclimate to the planet and settle in." My tone is stiff. The idea of her going to another master—or masters, is impossible. But there's been no opportunity for me to talk in private with Benn, to determine our plans. I'm past my anger and I want her more than ever. I just don't know if he feels the same way.

"I see." She purses her lips and crosses her legs.

I want to comfort her, but as the craft touches down, whisper soft—Zandians awaiting us on the pad, the door hissing open—suddenly Taxx has Danica. And he's holding a stunner to her head.

"This craft is now mine." His voice trembles, but his hand is tight on Danica's arm. "You are getting off, and then I am going to take it."

"Drop your weapon!" Benn's voice is harsh. "I don't know how the *veck* you got that out of the storage, but toss it down. *Now.*" He has his weapon out, trained on Taxx, his eyes fierce.

"Not unless you want her dead." Taxx's voice is fast. "I'll kill her in a second if the two of you don't step off this craft."

Panic and anger rise as I see terror on Danica's face. She's breathing shallow little gasps of air.

"Let her go!" I roar, stepping forward, drawing my own stunner, but stop in my tracks when Taxx puts the gun to her neck.

"A blast here will incapacitate her without killing her," he says, his voice flat. His hand trembles and I swear I see pain in his eyes.

I put up my hands. "Don't hurt her. Why are you doing this?" Adrenaline makes me alert to every sound, every movement.

"Get off the craft." His hand trembles. "I need it. And I need her."

"Why do you need it? Let her go and we'll talk." I step forward.

His eyes are wild. "Do you think she'd go blind from a Level 3 burst? Should we see? Maybe she'd just lose some

95

nerve function. Still be a sellable slave, though. Maybe even more desired, depending on who's buying."

His voice cracks and his hand trembles again. Danica squeaks and shakes, and I lock eyes with her, trying to communicate without words.

"Brother, we're not going to let you leave with her and this craft." Benn's voice is calm. "You know that, and we know that. Let her go and we can negotiate."

Taxx's hand wobbles, and I know we have one chance. I need Danica to duck down the same instant I leap forward. If only she could read my mind—

Taxx looks up and doesn't move. It's like he can't, or something—like he's literally turned to stone. He opens his mouth, and I swear, it's like he's pushing against an immovable force. At the same second, Danica moans and clenches her fists, like she's concentrating, and then—by the stars!—she ducks.

Benn and I spring forward and disarm him in a second. I tug Danica into my arms, touching her face, her hair as she swoons, limp. "Are you all right? Breathe. Breathe, baby, breathe." I panic until she gasps and her eyes fly open.

To my side, I see Zandians rush onto the craft and cuff Taxx, tug him to his feet.

"No!" Taxx screams, and collapses into a pile. I have never heard a Zandian sob, and the sound is as distressing as it is confusing. "I need it. I need it!" He appears utterly unhinged.

There's a thousand other voices, but the only one I want to hear is hers. Benn is right beside me.

"Talk to me, Danica." I lean forward until my forehead

is on hers, my horns tangling in her hair. "Tell me you're all right. Please, baby." I grab her face with both my hands. "You've got to be okay. Please. Please."

Benn puts both hands onto her shoulders. "Danica, we're here. We've got you."

She blinks, then touches her belly, her lips, her face. As if checking she's still there, alive. She sighs, and gives me a small smile and reaches back to put one of her hands on top of Benn's. "I'm fine."

I shoot a look at Benn, and I know without hesitation that he agrees. It's the expression on his face, powerful concern, fear and affection.

"Danica." I touch her cheek. "We want you to be our mate. Benn and I. We don't want a Zandian female."

"Are you sure?" Her voice trembles.

Benn comes to stand beside me. He swipes her hair off her neck and gives her a kiss on the exposed skin. "We want you."

She sucks in her breath and one tear forms in the corner of her eye. She looks from me, to Benn, and back again.

When Benn nods, I squeeze her hand. "Danica?"

She bites her lip. "Yes. I want you, too. Both of you. I say yes."

∾

Danica

. . .

KING ZANDER SCARES me with his direct gaze; it's like he knows all of my secrets. Thank God my deepest ones aren't encoded in the lines lasered into my skin.

"Danica." His voice is deep and authoritative. "Do you agree to take Gorde and Benn as your mates, and dedicate yourself to rebuilding Zandia for yourselves and your young?"

I glance at the huge males beside me. "Yes, my lord. I do."

"And you?" He looks at Gorde and Benn. "You choose her?"

They both agree, each stepping forward. Gorde puts a hand on my arm and Benn touches the small of my back.

My legs are shaky but I grab their hands in mine, strong hands. Powerful. Protective. How long will it be before they figure me out? Until then, I can live here. Grow stronger. Make plans.

I just better not fall in love.

"Then you will give her your crystals," King Zander proclaims. "Serve as her sponsors and take care of her. Ensure she is happy and satisfied."

"We will." Gorde squeezes my hand, his voice firm.

I glance at Benn. After all, he was the one who kept talking about a Zandian female. But his smile is full of affection when he looks at me, and his voice is strong. "Yes, Danica. We will."

"You will get a home in the capital city. Similar to this." King Zander taps on his comm device, and scrolls to a screen. He shows it to us: A sleek, efficient domicile in a vast urban area.

I'm surprised it's not a dome in the country. In the

holos I watched, I saw the homesteads where Zandians and humans were rebuilding the overmined land.

"Gorde and Benn are warriors," King Zander says. "They serve the throne running missions, so it doesn't make sense to base your unit anywhere else but the city."

"How will I serve, my lord?" I curtsy. My stomach churns with nerves.

"We will assess your skills and assign you to an area of your choosing." Zander taps his comm again and shows me a picture. "This is Arabel. She'll meet with you and help you get started." He pauses. "Of course, you will take the time you need to raise your young, when you have them."

I swallow hard. "Young. Yes."

Gorde slaps Benn on the back. "Starting the family unit. Now there's a mission I can't wait to run."

The two of them chuckle, and Benn leans in to kiss my cheek. "Sorry," he whispers. "But it's true. You're irresistible. I can't wait to see your belly swell with our young."

King Zander clears his throat.

I curtsy, keeping my voice steady. "Thank you."

"Thank you, Danica," he says, his eyes sincere. "Without your help, Zandia cannot reach its former strength and beauty."

CHAPTER 9

 anica

"My own home." I run my finger along the glass window that overlooks the capital city, staring into the bright hot light, the new domes of glass and steel. We arrived the planet rotation before and, because of our mating, were assigned this incredible domicile.

I turn to include Gorde and Benn. "Our home." I flush. "I can't believe it."

Akron was wealthy, but the comfort and wealth of his palace didn't extend to his sex slaves. I slept on a wooden pallet with no blanket for covering. Here, the sleep platforms are floating oval disks, covered in soft bedding. Everything is colorful and made of fine materials. I feel like royalty.

I touch my earlobe, where a crystal tingles. Their crystals.

"It doesn't hurt?" Benn reaches out and tugs my lobe, then runs his hand down my arm. "Here…or here?" He slides his hand under my loose Zandian shirt and cups my breast, tapping the nipples.

I suck in a breath, as arousal spirals through me. "It feels good."

"It will feel even better," Gorde promises, and lowers his voice to speak into my ear, "When we *veck* you. At the moment of climax, the crystals will add additional…encouragement."

"Mmm." I close my eyes as Gorde reaches down to cup my ass through my flowing skirt, then slides it down my body. Tugs down my panties. I help him by stepping out of them. "That sounds intriguing."

"Indeed." Gorde chuckles. "Benn, let's take off the rest of her garments and show her."

"Excellent plan." Benn pulls at the hem of my shirt. "Arms up, love, so I can remove this."

I lift my arms. "I thought I wasn't a slave anymore." I suck in my breath as the silky fabric skims my breasts and the cool air caresses my nipples.

"Certainly not." Benn bites my neck, tossing the fabric to the side. "Except in the bedroom."

"Because you like it when we master you here." Gorde pulls me into his body from behind, so my ass cups his cock, already hard through his pants. He palms both of my breasts and squeezes softly. "Am I not correct?"

I suck in a breath. "I may need to be reminded." I push my hips back, grinding into his heat. "Of how nice it can be. Then I'll let you know if I want to be your love slave."

I reach back and wind my hands up, into his thick hair and grab his horns.

He growls and gets harder. "Danica, don't do that yet." He pinches my nipples, just enough of a bite to make me moan with desire.

"This?" I do it again. "But why ever not?"

In a move so fast I don't see it coming, he whirls me around and then next thing I know, he's sitting on the sleepdisk and I'm over his lap. He slaps my ass, and the crack echoes around the chamber.

"Because you'll wait until you're told," he murmurs, giving me another spank. "Is that clear?"

"Ow," I complain, restless, letting my thighs part. "That hurts." I lift up my hips in silent encouragement.

He laughs. "Why do I think you like it?"

I wiggle my ass. "I don't know. Maybe because you can see...this?" I part my legs further and tilt my hips. "Mmm?"

"*Veck*, let me see it." Benn's voice is hoarse with need. The bed indents with his weight and then his hands run up my calves, my thighs. I whimper as he finds my core with his fingers and teases me, in and out. "She's so wet."

"Our naughty little mate likes her punishment," suggests Gorde.

"Then we should certainly oblige her with more. Hold her hands while I spank her pretty little ass pink." Benn puts both hands onto my ass cheeks and presses down softly, then traces circles on my skin. "I'll make her wiggle over our laps before we let her come."

I moan. "No, don't."

"I think she means *please*." Gorde laughs. "Look at how she grew even wetter when you said that." He runs his palms over my back and up to my shoulders. "Arms back, love, yes, like that." He arranges my hands in the small of my back and holds both of them in one of his. "See how nicely you're restrained now? Benn can spank you just as much as he likes and you can't get away."

My breasts push into his thighs, and the pressure on the crystals makes intense pangs of need vibrate into my nipples, and a matching sensation grows in my clit. "Oh!" I gasp, clenching my hands tighter.

He strokes my fists with his thumb. "Yeah? Feels good?"

"Gorde." The tenderness of his touch slays me.

"Danica." I hear the smile in his tone. "Relax and let us take care of you the way you need. I promise you can trust us."

I relax my fists and he reaches underneath me, and I lift up one side so he can more easily reach my breasts with those magic fingers. The instant he closes his thumb and forefinger over my nipple, I cry out, because at the same time, Benn spanks me, hard, right across both cheeks.

"Mother Earth." I can only gasp out the words as the two of them work my body in unison, playing my nipples, spanking my ass, until the need is so intense that I cry out their names.

"Benn, Gorde, please!"

"You want us to *veck* you?" Benn runs his hands, both of them, up my inner thighs, and cups my ass. "Tell us."

"Yes, please, right now," I encourage, twisting my hips.

"Who are your masters? Tell us." Gorde squeezes my nipples harder, a bite of pain that works with Benn's fingers to make me insane.

"You are! You both. Benn, Gorde, Master Gorde. Master Benn." I'm nearly incoherent.

"That's right. We are." Benn slaps my ass at the base of my thighs. "And look how nice and red she is, Gorde. She's ready for our cocks."

"Should we let her choose who goes first?" Benn slides a finger along my slit and drives it into me.

"No, I want both. At the same time." I gasp as he pushes deeper. "Master Benn. Please?"

His hand stills. "You sure?"

"Yes." All of us hear the conviction in my voice, I'm sure of it. "I need you both, right now."

"Your wish is our command, love." Benn picks me up and holds me in his arms. "Gorde?"

He quirks a brow at his friend, and Gorde smiles. "Got it." He lies down on the sleepdisk, his cock jutting up, hard and thick. "You're gonna ride me, Danica, like a good little slave. And once you get so hot you're ready to come, Benn's going to slide right into your nice, tight ass, so we can both *veck* you at once."

Benn slaps my ass once, then lifts me up. "Spread, love. Get your pretty thighs nice and wide so I can watch his cock slide into your pussy."

He puts me down next to Gorde, and I crawl over, toss one leg over him and position myself, breasts swinging, breath coming fast. "Like this?" I look over my shoulder to see Benn's eyes glittering with desire, then turn back to stare into Gorde's face. His expression, both fierce and tender, melts my heart, and as I slide myself down onto his magnificent cock, tears come to my eyes.

He reaches up to brush my cheek. "No crying, sweet slave," he murmurs. "This is a moment for pleasure." He puts both hands onto my hips. "Ride me, Danica. Ride my cock and make your pussy feel good."

He slaps my ass once and I whimper.

"You sore?" He smiles as I nod. "Good. Next time we'll spank you harder, too."

This makes me gush new moisture, and he groans, his eyes fluttering shut. "*Veck*, baby. I love that you like it rough. Yeah, like that."

I move up and down along his perfect cock, enjoying the feeling of power that comes with being on top, the one in charge. I allow his cock to brush my clit once, then again, then move so that I'm using him for my pleasure, not even taking him into me fully, but just rubbing my body along his to maximize the sensation.

"Oh!" My breath comes out in a gasp as Benn grabs my shoulders from behind. His cock is rock hard as he pulls me back into his body, his legs spread across Gorde's.

"You ready for me?" he murmurs, squeezing my breasts.

I lean back into his hard chest, enjoying his strong arms, the muscles moving as he holds me. His cock presses into the seam of my ass.

"Yes." I reach behind me to grab his horns and this time there's no complaint, just his growl of pleasure. His horns harden at my touch and I laugh with delight. "You like that."

"Gonna like this even more." He softly presses me forward, away from his chest. "Ride Gorde again, baby, and stick that ass out nice and high."

"With pleasure, Master." I'm so wet that I slide easily down onto Gorde's hard cock, smiling at his grunt of pleasure. I wiggle my body so my ass is arranged and spread my thighs, my breath coming faster. "It's...will it hurt?" A momentary concern makes me look back to check his face. But he's smiling. "Face forward," he reminds me.

A bottle clicks and warm oil runs down my ass cleft. Benn rubs it into my body, pushing his finger into my body just a bit, then deeper as I relax into his touch.

"Just enough to make it even better," he promises, drizzling more oil down my body, rubbing it into my ass. "And then it will make you scream with delight."

I clench my pussy on Gorde's cock, and clench my ass tight down on Benn's finger, already enjoying the double pleasure.

"Not yet," he warns, and gives me a sharp slap on my ass. "Right now you stay open, little human. Open nice and wide for my fingers, or how else will I get this huge cock into you?"

I moan but obey, allowing my muscles to go slack as he adds a second oiled finger to the first. "You see?" He pumps them in and out. "How it gets easier. How *vecking* good it feels."

"Mmmm." I push down onto Gorde's cock. "I'm almost ready—"

"No," Benn snaps and slaps my ass with his other hand and I clench again. He punctuates each word with a slap. "You. Will. Wait. For. Permission."

I moan. "But I need to."

"Oh, is that so?" He spanks again. "You come before you're told, little slave, and we'll take the belt to you until you can't sit tomorrow. Is that what you want?"

"No!" But his words inflame me, and now it's harder to hold back. "Gorde, Benn!"

"Keep that ass open," he warns, and presses the tip of his thick cock to my ass. "Because you only get to come once we're both buried balls deep in you. Is that clear?"

"Yes…" I moan, and the sounds turns to a hiss of pain as he pushes into me, inch by inch. It's excruciating, and I can't take more, until suddenly my body releases the tension and he slides in. I'm impossibly full, but it doesn't hurt anymore, and the excitement at this development drives me wild. I move, tentative at first, pulsing my pussy on Gorde's cock, lightly. Then harder. Each time I press my muscles together, I clench on two cocks, and as they press into me, on all the right places, my orgasm grows in a new way. It's something I've never felt before, the sensation blooming from so deeply inside me I can't breathe.

"Mother Earth…" I whisper, digging my nails into Gorde's back, clenching my toes along with my cunt. "I can't…I can't…"

Benn pulls out just an inch, then drives back in gently. Gently. Then hard. I scream at the sensation; it's too much and not enough.

Gorde grabs my hips. "Danica, ride me while he *vecks* your ass. Now."

I tremble, and the rhythm builds as the three of us become one entity. It's a slow dance as I go down onto Gorde's cock, then back onto Benn's, back and forth. Their hands are all over me, pulling, tugging, squeezing. My pussy and ass are on fire with desire and I'm calling out words, names, invocations. As the feeling grows, there's no holding back, no waiting for permission.

I scream and tighten all my muscles and explode into the most glorious orgasm of my entire life, my body on fire with joy. Each nerve ending vibrates with pleasure, the most incredible thing possible. It's like I can see the entire universe behind my closed lids, all the colors of the stars, the galaxies.

And as I come and come, pulsing with the joy of our union, both of my mates come, too. They roar out my name and grab my body, all of us sweaty and hot, the moment taking us all from three to one. I fear I've fallen for both of them, irrevocably. Mother Earth, I think I'm in love. What will happen when they discover my secret?

∼

Benn

"I can't believe it's already been four weeks." I clip my combat belt to my waist and glance at Gorde who's adjusting the flight coordinates inside our craft. Outside the window, the purple sun rises large on the horizon, a sight that never fails to make me swell with pride: Zandia.

He glances over at me and grins. "Four perfect weeks with our new little human."

"You're glowing like a imploding star." I roll my eyes, but can't help smiling back. "She is *vecking* amazing, I have to admit it."

"No regrets?" He raises an eyebrow, and looks away briefly to talk into his comms unit. "Lifting off in five." He turns back to me. "At all?"

I shake my head. "I'm content." I tilt my head, surprised at my own admission. "With our little human."

"Good." He slaps the console. "And speaking of little... have you noticed?" He touches his stomach. "I think she's not so little anymore."

I lean forward. "I thought so too." Excitement courses through my body. "A young, Benn. Ours." I punch one fist into my other hand. *"Veck."* It's exciting, but nerve-wracking as well.

He notes my expression. "If we can do this"—he waves a hand around our high-tech craft—"surely we can take care of a tiny little creature." He winces. "Who needs everything."

I swallow. "She didn't say anything to us. Surely she knows?" A wave of unease hits me. Danica still has secrets. She won't talk about her past master, and sometimes she gets this look in her eyes—a distant stare, and closes up entirely.

He shrugs. "She must. If we can see it..."

I frown. "Are they supposed to grow that fast? It's only so recent."

He shrugs. "I think each human is different. We need

to take her to Dr. Daneth, make sure everything is progressing correctly."

"As soon as we get back." My pulse pounds. "Do you think it's yours, or mine?"

"I don't know. Whoever is first, we'll make sure the other is second." He crosses his arms. "That's fair, right?"

I nod. "Yes." I push back my competitive urges. "Either way, as long as it's healthy."

"A Zandian." He stands up and beams. "It's what we planned, and it's happening. By the stars."

I nod. "We're doing what's right for the planet." I've never felt like this before. The pride that swells inside my chest is larger than anything I've felt.

My comm beeps with new information on our latest mission and I sigh, then turn my attention back to work. "Now sit down and focus, because if we find another one like Taxx, we're going to need to have all of our energy."

Gorde groans and sits down hard into the nearest console chair. "That excrement. Has he said yet why he did it?"

I shake my head. "He's in detention and isn't talking. It's a *vecking* shame."

"I have no sympathy." He snaps the words, and his eyes narrow. "He almost hurt Danica, and he's a traitor to Zandia." He curls his fists. "I'd like to rip him apart myself."

I nod. "Wonder what happened to him to make him turn like that."

"Not every Zandian is worthy." His words are clipped. "Do you think King Zander should enable the death penalty?" The king has long refused to spill Zandian blood on account of our population's near extinction.

The idea turns me cold inside. "He's still our brother, on some level. I don't know. Let's go over our recon plans."

He nods. "Agreed." Then he turns to me, after a pause. "During the struggle. Did it seem like…"

"Like what?" Something in his tone makes me peer more closely at his face.

"I don't know." He makes a low growl. "When Taxx had the stunner to her neck. She needed to duck down, and he needed to stop moving. And then it happened, both things, right at the exact time. Then you and I disabled him in an instant."

I frown, replaying it in my mind, even though the images are jarring, unwanted. "It's our bond. How well we work together." I shrug.

He shakes his head and his brow wrinkles. "It was like Danica was working with us, too."

I consider this, and remember Taxx groaning, as if he were stuck under a heavy slab of metal, and how I knew without hesitation that this was the moment to strike. "Perhaps it just means that the three of us are fated to be together. We work well as a team." It certainly felt right to save her, and it was in that moment I knew I needed her as mine, forever.

"I suppose that's true." He smiles.

I roll my eyes. "Now please, can we focus on the mission?"

~

I'M FRUSTRATED—OUR trip came up empty, and all we got for our troubles was a narrow escape from Ocretion airspace with our cover intact. But as soon as I see Danica, my anger and irritation at the day melts away.

"You look beautiful." I lean in to kiss her soft pink lips, lingering to taste the flavor that bursts onto my tongue. "And you're delicious." I lick my tongue along her mouth and slap her ass.

She giggles. "It's grapes." She flushes. "I'm still trying out so many new foods." We have new Earth-based foods delivered to her almost every planet rotation.

"I'd almost eat every planet rotation too, if I could taste it from your mouth." I tug her in for another kiss.

Beside me, Gorde growls. "Don't be greedy, brother."

She moves easily into his arms, and presses both hands to his cheeks, looking up into his eyes. "I missed you." She smiles, and he melts, his dour look transforming into one of fascination.

I laugh, even as I know I'm just as whipped. One smile from our human and we're all hers, entirely. And I like it.

"Both of us…" I reach out and touch her belly. "Missed both of you. Am I right?" I hold my breath.

Her face goes pale. "I…" She steps back from Gorde's embrace, her hands falling to her sides.

"Danica, it's all right." I reach out and touch her arm, which has gone cold.

"It's better than all right," growls Gorde. "It's fantastic. It's what we wanted from the very beginning. Our own young!" He tilts his head to peer at her. "What's wrong?"

She stares, then shakes her head, a quick snap. "I should have told you as soon as I, ah, knew. I was processing it. I'm sorry; I'm...really excited." Her face looks anything but.

Cold unease presses onto my chest, and I push it back. "Are you nervous? Dr. Daneth says humans bear Zandian young well, and you will have the best medical support during the...process." I wave my hand, unsure of which words to use.

She blinks and bites her lip. "The idea of a baby. It's like nothing I've ever experienced." Her eyes well up.

Gorde pulls her into his arms. "This is the best day. We have you, and now a young on the way. This is exactly what Zandia needs—what we all need." His face glows and his eyes are lit up with joy. "Just look at us for one moment and you'll see that this is everything we've dreamed of. The culmination of a lifetime of plans."

He speeds up as he speaks, stroking her shoulders. "You're ours more than ever, now. This cements us together forever."

She shivers. I reach out to touch her hair, place my hand on her neck in what I hope is a comforting touch. "You don't need to worry about a single thing. This Zandian baby, and you, will be kept safe from all ugliness and all predators." I know she's still probably terrified about being on auction, her escape, all the creatures who would harm her. "I will personally kill any foreign being who threatens you or Zandia. Is that clear?" My voice rises with passion.

Danica stills. She takes a breath. "Completely." Her smile seems forced. "Let's go to the sleepdisk." She takes my hand and Gorde's. "I want to feel you inside me now. Please."

And as we make love, both of us taking turns to make her cry out in pleasure, I sense a strange difference in her, something I can't understand. So I double my efforts, bringing her as much passion as I possibly can, enough to drown out the little voice of doubt in my head.

CHAPTER 10

G orde

BESIDE ME, Danica vibrates with energy. Her foot taps fast and she clenches her fingers together as Bayla runs the scan over her bare belly. "What do you see?" Her voice is taut.

"Relax." The midwife's voice is soothing, but Danica squeezes my fingers harder than ever.

"There's the heart." Dr. Daneth points to the screen, where a pulsing blob of white and black motion blurs in front of my eyes.

I peer forward, my heart leaping to match the pulse of the tiny thing. "It's so small." I hear the wonder in my own tone.

Dr. Daneth chuckles. "Actually, it's quite big for the

time frame." He blinks. "Growing faster than expected. If this growth rate keeps up"—he shoots a look at his mate—"Bayla, can you pull up the chart?"

She nods and a hologram springs into the air between us. The doctor gestures. "If we assume a linear curve to the enlargement rate, the young will be approximately forty-five percent larger than a typical Zandian baby by the end of gestation time, and we may have to consider alternative birthing procedures."

"Which are what?" Danica twists to look at him, eyes wide.

I press her hand as Bayla soothes, "Danica, it's completely safe for the young. If necessary, we'll make a small surgical incision—"

"You'll slice me open?" Her face has gone pale and she trembles. "No, you can't. You can't. You can't…" She struggles to sit up, grabbing Benn's hand as well for leverage.

Dr. Daneth and Bayla shoot each other a look, just as I snap, "Cut her open? By the stars…"

"She'll heal!" Bayla raises her voice to be heard over all of us. "Please, listen. She'll be fine. We've done it before. We provide medication to mitigate the pain, and it's a simple surgery."

Danica relaxes. "I'll…heal?" She blinks and lowers herself back down.

Dr. Daneth clears his throat. " It won't hurt, Danica. You and the young will be fine. The recovery will take a few weeks, but you'll be back to normal in a short period. We don't even know if it's necessary."

"Oh. I…oh." She takes a deep breath and touches her stomach. "All right. I understand."

"Were things different elsewhere? What's going on?" I lean in, concerned. "Tell us."

She shakes her head. "I misunderstood, that's all. I thought…"

"Danica, it is not in any being's best interest to hurt you." Dr. Daneth's voice is taut. He's still learning how to interact with humans. His mate helps, but sometimes he's awkward. "We'll take care of you and the Zandian young."

She nods. "Can we go now?" She looks from Benn to me, a pleading expression on her face. This time when she sits up, she swings her legs over the side of the examination table.

I look at the doctor, who nods. "Eat additional food when hungry. Humans need extra energy when carrying young. More rest, too. See me again in three weeks."

Danica is already grappling with her clothing and seems not to have heard him. I touch her face, and she flinches, then blinks.

"Did you catch that?" I stroke her hair. "About the food?"

She nods. "Yes, Master."

She steps to the door, then turns back. "Thank you." She clears her throat and darts forward. Benn follows, but as I turn on my heel, the doctor touches my shoulder.

"A moment." He looks toward Danica and Benn, who are already many paces ahead, then back at me. "In private?"

"What is it?" I want to be with my mate, and I'm irritated at this delay.

119

The doctor lowers his voice. "The brain scan on this fetus is unusual."

"And?" Icy dread trickles down my back. "Does that mean something is wrong with the young?" I step forward, adrenaline spiking, peering at the muddled picture frozen on the screen. The details mean nothing to me, other than the important one: It's my young. My future.

"I don't know." His voice is stiff. "Human-Zandian young are still rare, and we don't know everything. This may be fine. I'd like to keep a closer eye on her progress, though." He pulls up the brain scan holos. A frown spreads across his face.

"Bayla?" I can hear the pleading tone to my voice as I turn to the midwife.

She doesn't meet my eyes. "Every gestation is different. Just make sure she's eating and resting appropriately."

I nod. "Can I do anything else?" I hate feeling helpless.

"Don't worry her," Bayla says, after a short pause.

"So this is a secret?" I raise my voice, stomach churning.

Dr. Daneth puts his hand out. "Additional anxiety in humans is not healthy for the young. There is no need to worry her. But"—he tilts his head and looks at me, as if trying to say something I won't quite understand—"I'd like to do a little more analysis on these brain scans and see if I can answer some questions I have."

I breathe out. "What do mean, questions?" I clench my fists. His attitude is making me both scared and angry.

He shakes his head. "I'll let you know as soon as I

complete my review." He raises his hand and strides from the room.

"It will probably be fine." Bayla turns to clean the sono module, her movements quick and concise. She gives me a small smile, but it doesn't meet her eyes. "We'll see you soon."

~

WHEN I REJOIN Benn and Danica at our hovercraft, her face has regained color and she's laughing. He smiles down at her, and for a moment I'm focused just on the three of us, our family, forgetting the doctor's words.

"What did he want?" Benn glances over as he helps Danica up the steps into the craft, touching her ass as he does.

"Just reminded me about food." I swallow hard.

Benn tilts his head and gives me a quizzical look. He knows me too well. Zandians believe it's dishonorable to lie, but I haven't lied. I just didn't tell the whole truth. I shake my head—*not now.*

"All right." His voice is easy, but he frowns before he turns back to Danica with a grin. "Come on, then, human. Let's get you home. I think we need to do some practice on building the next young."

~

Danica

. . .

THE LOVEMAKING, as usual, is phenomenal. During it, I forget everything but the pleasure, moments of perfect bliss that almost make up for the worries consuming me.

Afterward, I feel the need to stay busy to keep the thoughts at bay. I get up and dress, leaving my two mates lazing on the sleepdisk, sated expressions on their faces, and head to my crafting bench.

"I've been working on something new." I pick up my latest creation and turn it over in my hands, examining the wires and metal. I compare it to the schematic on the comms unit, a flashing blue and silver digital map, and frown. The layout is acceptable, but I think I could reduce the amount of space needed if I moved the charging capacitor over—

"What is that?" Gorde, ever attentive, glances over.

"It's a phaser." I flush.

"What do you know about those?" His voice holds nothing negative—no contempt or anger. It's just a question, but to answer it requires information I can't quite explain.

"Nothing, when I started." I put it down. "Drayn showed me how he's building them, and as soon as I saw it, something just clicked in my brain. Like I automatically understood how they go together. So, because I need to do something, I offered to try and improve it."

"But in your past you never did any tech work, right?" Gorde gets up and saunters over. I catch my breath at his naked torso, his cock impressive even now that he's not erect, his thighs powerful.

"You know I was a sex slave." I look back at the device in my hands. "No, I never had the chance."

"And yet you"—he pauses. He knows I don't like discussing my past. Refuse to—"have already learned to cipher?" his voice holds surprise.

I stick up my chin. I admit my ability to learn lately seems enhanced, but I'm not going to discuss that fact with my mates. "Bayla said humans learn fast, once we are given the chance. Yes. I did learn to cipher."

"By the stars," he muses, admiration written into his expression. "Do you know how long it takes Zandian children?"

"I'm no child." I turn away, rubbing my belly.

"I know that. It's just remarkable a being with no experience can do it so quickly." There's something in his tone I can't quite place.

"Are you jealous?" I tease. "Feeling threatened by the clever little human?" I flip the device. "Who can learn Zandian tech so quickly that it makes you worried?"

He crosses his arms. "Threatened by a human? Not likely." He scoffs. But then he touches my arm and his expression softens. "And you amaze me—us, every day. Absolutely."

I shrug, glancing again at the digilayout. "We humans are actually pretty intelligent." It's true. On Zandia, I've come to find humans have skills at logical analysis and a vast, untapped creativity that—when unleashed—seems unstoppable. Bayla even told me, in an undertone, that some Zandians and humans are both starting to think that humans may even rival Zandians in intellectual ability. Once we are fully trained, there's no telling what our capabilities will be.

I pick up my robotweeze and try to insert the cap into

the new location, but it's a tight squeeze. I frown and without warning and a small spark, the thing is complete in my hands.

I squeak and drop it onto the table, fingers trembling.

"Danica?" Gorde steps closer. "You okay?"

I take a deep breath and nod. "I'm fine." There's no mistaking it this time. I made it move with my mind. I touch my stomach and the creature inside stirs, either a kick or a press of the arm. I push back, and the baby presses again, as if sensing me and reacting. I repeat the action, and the young presses once again. *Asking me. Telling me.*

I put my other hand to my mouth and Gorde sees my face.

"Is it the young? It's moving?" He strides closer. "Is he kicking?"

He comes forward and presses his hand to my belly. "Can I feel it?" His voice is reverent, and I think I see something else, though—a kind of worry, or anxiety. But he sounds excited enough. "Danica—he's moving! Benn, get over here!"

"She." The word comes out automatically as Benn jogs up and touches my belly.

"Dr. Daneth said it's too early to tell." Benn's strong hand moves across my stomach. "He's active."

"It's a girl. I can tell." The feel of their two hands on my belly, protective, gentle, brings tears to my eyes.

"Most Zandian young are males," Gorde cautions me.

"I can tell." *She told me.*

"We'll see." Benn seems unconvinced.

I bite my lip. Yes, we certainly will. But what we'll see…that's something I can't be sure of. I need to tell them the truth now, but when I look at their faces, so full of love and eager anticipation, the words stick in my throat. And I say nothing.

CHAPTER 11

I'M HERE. Don't hurt me. I'm here. Big round eyes, a sweet face. *Don't hurt me. Don't let them hurt me.* Hand grabbing her, tearing her away from me. Blood.

I gasp and sit up in bed, panting, sweat dripping from my forehead, a strangled cry dying in my throat. I put both hands onto my swelling belly, making sure everything is still okay.

Gorde is awake in an instant. "Danica!" He grabs me. "You're burning up."

He wipes my forehead. "You never sweat this much. Benn, get her fluids."

Benn, too, is alert instantaneously—they're warriors, always ready to react—and he comes over with a water container for me.

I gulp the cool liquid, then start to cry.

"It was a nightmare." Gorde pulls me to his body, stroking my arm. "It's all right." His hands are warm and calming, but I can't relax.

"It was so real." I'm shaking.

"What was it? Memories of your previous master?" Benn touches my shoulder.

"Yes." I lie. "Please, I just want to relax." *Don't let them hurt me.* I cry out and grab his hands. "Hold me. Just hold me, please?"

"Tomorrow we'll take her to Dr. Daneth." Gorde's voice is low as he strokes me. "Danica, your nightmares are getting worse. It can't be good for you or the baby."

"I know." My voice is muffled, talking into his chest.

"So let us help you." His voice is taut. "If you tell us about your past, we won't judge. We can help you."

I shake my head. "I need more time."

He blows out a breath. "What happens when we run out of time?"

I stiffen in his arms. What, indeed? "I'm sorry, but I'm not ready."

He slides me over to Benn and stands up. I hate that my reticence is driving a wedge between us, but right now, I'm giving all I can.

"There are other humans here with difficult pasts. Maybe talking to one of them will help."

He paces the chamber, then when I don't respond, he curses under his breath. "I'm going to exercise."

"At this hour?" Benn raises his eyebrows.

"I need to clear my head." Gorde disappears out the door.

In the sudden silence, the only thing I hear is my

breathing and Benn's, but when I concentrate, I hear everything: the creaks of the building, and Gorde's footfalls, already half a mile distant, his strong feet crunching down on the blue Zandian gravel along the footpath. A night bird trills, something lonely in high notes, leaves rustling softly around it. Finally Gorde runs out of my auditory range, and I shudder.

"What?" Benn grasps me. "Danica?"

How can I tell him that I'm changing into something else—something un-human—day by day? I shake my head. "I'm fine."

WHEN SHE SEES ME, Bayla's face goes into an *oh* of surprise. "Danica! Come in. I wasn't expecting you." She glances at my abdomen.

"Hi." I swallow hard and enter her chamber. "I wanted to talk with you."

"Of course." She smiles at me. "Would you like some tea? Our queen is growing chamomile now, an old Earth botanical that is soothing for expectant mothers." She gestures to her cabinet.

"She'd prefer water," I say automatically, the knowledge coming to me without pause. Then, at Bayla's expression, I cough and amend it to, "I mean, I'd prefer water, right now."

She hands me a container. "You're big for this stage of pregnancy. Feeling tired?"

I nod.

We sit in silence for a few minutes while I drink my

water and listen to her heartbeat and the blood whooshing through her veins, a soothing sound that I've learned to put into the background.

"What did you want to ask?" Bayla's face is guarded but kind.

I shrug. "I was curious about the birthing process in general." I swallow. "I watched the holograms, but..." I bite my lip. "Have you any experience with young that are not human-Zandian mixes?"

She smiles. "One Zandian-Zandian, as well. A Zandian female named Eslyn and her three mates were blessed with a young this solar cycle."

I nod. "Have you ever learned about other young? They stay pregnant for different time frames, right?"

She quirks a brow, and to my relief doesn't ask why I need to know. "Other beings have different gestation periods. For instance, the Tellurians have a gestation period of merely two months. But the Finn, it's seventeen." I shudder, thinking of the transport owner back on Hectan-3.

I nod and tap my foot. "Genes mix, right?"

She blinks. "What's your question, Danica?"

"What if, say"—I take a deep breath—"what if a cruel species mated with a nice species. Could the resulting offspring be...good?" I trail off, clenching one hand in the other.

She touches my knotted fingers. "Danica?"

I shake my head. "I'm just wondering. The whole thing is so amazing, you know?"

She sighs. "Well, anything is possible, I suppose. But without experience, it's impossible to predict."

"But what if the baby told the mother it was a good creature?"

"They can't do that." She squeezes my palm. "Not until they're far older. Are you nervous, Danica? I promise we'll take care of you and your young." But when she looks at me, I get that strange feeling again. The way she doesn't quite meet my eyes. What does she know? I was relieved that nobody commented after the sono, but soon enough, the truth will come out.

"I know you will." I sip the water. "I want to know what will happen. So I can be prepared."

"Let's go over it."

As she talks, showing me pictures, holding up supplies, I nod and pay close attention to what I'm going to need as a bare minimum to do this safely. By myself. Just in case it comes to that.

CHAPTER 12

 orde

"So Taxx still won't say anything?" I blow out my breath and turn to Master Seke, the old warrior who trained every surviving Zandian after our planet was invaded. He's a father figure to us. A mentor. His face looks more lined than usual, and I wonder if the pressures of keeping Zandia guarded are getting to him.

"He's gone mute." Seke strides to the window and looks out.

"I still don't understand why he wanted to take the ship, and Danica both." I frown. "We had just saved his life and brought him back to his homeland. What could be so compelling that'd he'd commit a high crime to immediately leave?"

Seke frowns. "My best guess is blackmail."

"How?" I glance over at him.

"I think he was being compelled to do it. But for what reason?" He crosses his arms.

"Why can't he just tell us?" My voice is sharp.

"Beings are rarely logical, even Zandians." The Master at Arm's voice is dry. "Upfront communication could solve so many problems."

"What could be more important than his own life?" I clench a fist. "He knows the death penalty is on the table for him." I shoot a glance at Seke. "Isn't that right?"

"It's been discussed, but King Zander will not execute a Zandian." Seke's voice is firm. "Not even for treason."

I nod. "But he's willing to live his entire life in prison?"

"It appears so." Seke folds his arms over his chest. "How is your new mate?"

My shoulders tighten. "Fine. The young is growing and she should deliver, Dr. Daneth said, in three lunar cycles."

The old warrior shoots me an expressive glance. "Yet you seem worried. Why?"

I shake my head. "She's moody. Night terrors. Closed off." I don't tell him what Dr. Daneth said about the infant's brain scan, or the size of the baby. The need to do more examination of the holos.

He flicks a brow. "Human females are sensitive and perplexing creatures, even without pregnancy hormones."

I think of her terror-stricken face the other day when she woke up from her nightmare. "I hope so."

Seke slaps me on the shoulder. "Another Zandian. It will be a day to celebrate."

"Balance out the numbers," I try to joke. "I brought in a bad one, so I'll give you a good one, a new one, to make up for it."

His hand presses into my arm. "No, Gorde. Never blame yourself. You had no control over Taxx's plans. You did what we asked, which was to rescue a Zandian. What he did after that is not your responsibility."

"I didn't watch him closely enough." Failure makes me so angry I could shout. "I failed her and Zandia. I didn't recognize the danger."

"Yet you reacted quickly, you and Benn, and were able to disarm him."

"Yes." My voice is uncertain. That moment is fixed in my mind forever—the look on Danica's face, almost like she knew what I wanted her to do. Then the way she bent down in concentration, and the way Taxx froze. More and more, I feel that she's hiding something big.

"Your training and your reflexes saved the situation." His voice is calm.

I'm not entirely convinced he's right, and I shake my head. "The whole thing was a mess."

He slaps my shoulder again. "Our life is going to be a series of messes and successes from here on out. This rebuilding isn't for the weak, Gorde. We will never be perfect. But we need to do our best, and keep moving forward." He looks into my face. "Do you understand? We make the best of what we have, and we use all of our resources."

I nod, encouraged. "I do. Thank you, Master."

"Thank you. Now get back out there and spend time with your mate before the young comes. I promise you that there will be few, ahem, moments"—he smiles—"for intimacy, when the young first arrives."

I smile, knowing he's right.

"I will. Thank you."

∼

Benn

"Come on," I urge Danica. "The light is fading, and I want you to see it before the sun sets."

"I just need a few things." She giggles at my eye roll; she likes it when I tease her.

"If I knew humans were so slow..." I throw up my hands.

"You'd have gotten down on the ground to beg me to show you how to properly savor each moment?" She raises an eyebrow and puts a fluid packet into her satchel. "If I knew Zandians were so intent on racing around all the time..."

I snatch her up in my arms and bury my face in her hair. That *vecking* glorious pale blonde hair, soft and fly-away, like moss. Like spray from a waterfall. Fragrant, delicate—like her. I speak into her neck. "Savoring how long it takes to prepare your snacks? *Veck*, baby, do you need the entire cupboard?"

"And then some." She squeals as I bite her neck. "You know how hungry I get these days." Before the visit to Dr. Daneth, she was tense. Afterwards, she eased up. I think she's getting acclimated to life here with us.

"That we do." Gorde steps back into the open door-way. "I think you eat the equivalent of an entire solar cycle's worth of produce." He strides forward and touches her belly, an affectionate smile on his face. "Not that we mind, of course." He points to the craft outside our home. "I have our ground transport ready. If you two can possibly force yourselves to leave for a few minutes, we may just make our destination in time."

"It's not my fault." Danica gives Gorde the sweetest smile, and bats her lashes. "Benn was being affectionate, and how can I say no to that?"

I slap her ass once, not hard, and she squeals. "Beast."

"That's right." I do it again, kiss her, then reluctantly put her down, trailing my hands over her arms, squeezing her palm, before letting her stand alone. "Your beast. And you love it."

"That I do." She reaches up on tiptoe to kiss me, her belly brushing my abdomen. A spark of passion and protective pride flows through me. My mate. My young.

She takes my hand then, and Gorde's, and the moment is complete. Her face is so vibrant and healthy, her eyes bright and shining—she's never been prettier. It's true what other Zandians say: There's something unmistakably beautiful about a pregnant human who's yours.

"So where are we going?" Danica steps into the craft and sits in her console chair, peering out the window as we set off, gliding quickly a few feet off the ground.

"You'll love it," I promise, and shoot a glance at Gorde. He looks back and smiles, but there's a guarded expression on his face, like there's something he's not telling me. Things have been a little off-kilter with him since our visit to Dr. Daneth. Danica is more relaxed; he's not. I wonder if he's concerned about whether the young is his or mine? After all, he was the one who liked Danica first... and fell for her hardest.

"We're here," he announces, when we arrive. The look on Danica's face tells me this was a great idea, because her eyes—so wide, and that smile? It's everything.

"I've never seen anything so gorgeous," she breathes. "What is this place?"

"It's called the Zandal Highlands." Gorde takes her hand to help her off the craft. "Upcountry that was untouched by the Finn. King Zander recently approved mated couples to request plots of land here."

"For a new home?" Danica reaches down to touch the grass, knee high and soft, waving in the breeze.

"No," I laugh, and touch her back. "For vacation spots. For pleasure."

"A place just for pleasure," she repeats, putting both hands on her belly. "Extraordinary."

"A place to come to relax." Gorde strides forward and points at the graceful trees. "Hear that?"

We all stop and listen, and he continues, "It's a stream. Crystal clear. You can drink from it. Swim in it."

"I never learned how to swim." Danica walks forward to examine the water, her eyes glowing. "It's not something that my old master..." She stops and presses her lips together.

"We'll teach you. And the young." I'm uncharacteristically excited. "I can just see his horns now, dipping into the water for the first time."

"*She*," Danica corrects me automatically.

"I know, you keep saying that, but Dr. Daneth says that most Zandian-human babies have been boys so far," I remind her. "Don't get your hopes up."

Danica's smile wavers, then strengthens. "Let's worry about that later." She touches my face, almost hesitant. "Right now I'd like to enjoy time with the two of you."

"That can be arranged." I slide my hand under her shirt and cup her breast. "Who are we to say no to our mate?"

I lower my lips to claim her mouth, but I can't push away the nagging thought. It's a pattern I should've noticed sooner.

Danica's distracting us from whatever's bothering her with sex.

ON THE DRIVE BACK, we're quiet, a comfortable silence. Danica hums to herself, a tune I don't recognize, not that I'm musically inclined.

"What is that melody?" I ask.

She stops abruptly. "I...don't know."

Gorde glances over. "Something you heard from other, ah, slaves, maybe?"

Danica shakes her head. "No, I-I can't recall where I heard it."

Our craft beeps and slows, and an automated chime rings out.

"*Veck.*" Gorde growls. "Looks like we're having an issue with the GPS controller module. I knew the mechanical team was putting the upgrades in before they were ready."

"Well, let's take a look." I sigh. "With all the work you

and I do on our fighter craft, I'm sure we can figure out a simple transport problem."

"We don't need to rely on the GPS," Danica points out. "We can just self-drive."

I fake a sigh of horror. "Don't say such a thing! We're on a relaxing day, Danica. Not a working trip. Please be sure to honor the difference."

"Oh, Master, my abject apologies." She giggles and pretends to bow to me. "Forgive me for insinuating that you should use a single brain cell on this pleasure outing."

"Apology accepted." I narrow my eyes, "If you agree to suck my hard cock later."

She purses her lips. "Hmmmm...agreed. If you, in return, lick me until I scream with pleasure."

I can't resist a smile from spreading across my face at the idea of her delicious pussy. "Definitely agreed."

Gorde already has the panel snapped open and extracts the module, a small device of silver and wires. "Here's the culprit." He turns it over. "I think."

Danica's at his side in an instant. "This isn't too different from the way we control charge capacitance on the phaser." Her voice is thoughtful, and she taps her cheek with her index finger.

"Oh?" Gorde raises his eyebrows and smiles.

She crosses her arms over her swelling belly. "Oh indeed." She scowls, then bursts into laughter. "Hand me a robotool and I'll show you how to fix it."

"Oh, you will?" I can't resist this, but at the same time, part of me is rooting for her to be right. I certainly don't know how to fix this on the fly—I'm sure I could figure it out, given enough time, but I'm curious to see if Danica really knows what she's talking about.

Gorde gives her the device and she bends over, her silky hair falling all over her shoulders.

"Let's see…" She frowns. "Oh, look. This wire has come loose." She points with the tip of the tool, and Gorde leans in, casually placing his hand on her ass as he does it.

She laughs and smacks his arms. "Pay attention. The lead isn't making consistent contact with the connection, which is why the control screen was cutting out intermittently. See?"

"I do see." But Gorde's looking at her face, not at the device. He's impressed, and so am I.

"I'll do it. You shouldn't be working with the solder material. There's lead in it, and that can't be good for developing young." I extract the tools I need from the cabinet. "Danica, you're—that's incredible." My heart is full.

She smiles and waves her hand, but a flush comes over her face and the smile that comes is a happy one. "It's nothing."

"It's not nothing." Gorde puts his arms around her. "A mate who's as beautiful as the Tellurian constellations, who bears our young, and who's also a genius? How did we get so lucky?" He touches her face. "We're the best team ever. The three happiest beings on this planet."

And as I reconnect the loose wire, fixing the connection so that the current flows through it the way it was meant to go, what I think to myself is that he's right. The three of us are inextricably linked, and when we're in sync —like in this moment—the energy that flows among us is the most remarkable thing I've ever felt.

CHAPTER 13

"So the other night?" Janette, a young human who lives in the dome beside ours, lowers her voice and puts her hand on my arm, leaning in. "My two mates tried this new...thing. And Mother Earth, was it fantastic!" Her whole face glows. I have to say—all the human females I've met on Zandia so far seem happy with their situations.

"Oh, have more strawberries. I grow them using a proprietary mix of fertilizer that I made myself." She points out back to her ecodome greenhouse, then pushes the basket over to me.

"These are so good." I cram another red berry into my mouth and it bursts into a symphony of flavor on my tongue. "Don't leave me hanging. What thing do you speak of?" I raise my eyebrows and give her a stern look. "Now I'm dying of curiosity."

She laughs and looks toward her sleepdisk. "So they got this device from Dr. Daneth that goes into my ass, like a plug, and it vibrates. With a cock in my pussy and that in my ass? Oh, the orgasm was phenomenal. You should get one for you and your mates." She nods, and glances across the room at her small twins, little human boys who are giggling and chattering together, planning mischief.

"Watch out for those two," I say, with a grin, before I think it through. "They're planning to climb the trellis outside the dome during their nap time, the one for the hibiscus vines. They think they can make a clubhouse up there out of discarded trans boxes."

"What?" She tilts her head. "How do you know that?"

My heart twists in my chest and I touch my belly. "Ah…I guess I heard them before?"

"When?" She leans forward. "They were across the room the whole time."

"Um." I think fast. "When you were on your comm, I think? They came a little closer. They didn't know I was listening, I guess."

"Oh. Well, it's not unexpected. They're such rascals." She laughs, but her face shows pride and joy. "I bet you can't wait for your own to be born. May I?" She hovers her hand over my stomach, and I nod. "Oh, the young is moving. I remember those moments." She sighs.

"I bet yours were pretty aggressive, though." I look over at the two boys, who are eyeing us with the look of children who are figuring out just how much they can get away with.

"They kicked my ribs so hard they almost dislocated one." She shakes her head. "But it was worth it. Dr. Daneth had to cut open my belly to take them out, but apparently it's not a complicated procedure, considering. And I healed just fine."

I shudder, thinking of Akron's claws, his cold eyes. Sweat breaks out on my brow and I wipe it away, taking a deep breath.

"They give you a medication so you feel nothing, Danica. I promise it. No pain at all, just pressure. And it's over in a blink—so fast! They stitch you up so effortlessly and the wound seals up, as if it was never there. If they need to do that, I'll come be by your side, all right?"

I grab her hand and nod, trying to compose myself. "Thank you."

When I forget about my past, everything and every being are so perfect, and I can trick myself into thinking this is mine forever. I feel such overwhelming love for this life: My mates. New friends. My freedom. Learning to cipher, allowing my brain to expand. Making love by the stream. The ability to eat a red berry bursting with sun and flavor, with a friend. Simple pleasures I could never have dreamed of, back serving Akron.

But I don't deserve these friends, my mates, this whole life. Everything is a lie. I thought coming here would buy me time, but all it's done is make me fall in love with everything...that I'll eventually have to give up.

"So I hear that you're doing great things with electronics. Do you want to join a math class I'll be teaching? I'm ready to start the calculus classes now, and I'm trying to get all of us human women enrolled." She pops another berry into her mouth.

"I'd like that." I smile at her, and pretend the future is secure. "That sounds perfect. Oh! Oh." I grab my belly. "That's...hmmm."

"Everything okay?" Janette cocks her head. "You're not due for a few months, right?"

"Yes." This wasn't a kick, it was more of a squeeze, a tight pressure. Like my body was clenching up. I take a deep breath and hold it, relieved when it doesn't happen a second time. "Just a momentary thing. I'm fine."

"I'm glad you're here." She squeezes my hand. "This life is so much more than I ever expected. And it keeps getting better."

~

Gorde

"You wanted to see me?" I knock on the half-open door, peering into Dr. Daneth's lab.

He turns and beckons. "Gorde. Come in." He frowns as I approach. "I need to talk to you about Danica's pregnancy."

"What is it?" My voice comes out rough from anxiety.

"Close the door." The doctor blinks his amethyst eyes and waits until I do so before he speaks again. "Gorde, I don't think the young is yours."

"It's Benn's?" I break out into laughter. "We talked

about it, and that's not a problem. Whichever one of us is the father will make sure that—"

"No. I mean it's neither of yours. Not Zandian at all." His voice is cool and even but I think I see a flicker of compassion cross his face.

"No, that can't be right." My blood boils. "Upon what grounds would you suggest that?" I step forward, growling.

"Stand back," he snaps, putting up a hand, and I immediately stop in my tracks. "I examined the sono in detail and used info mapping to create detailed 3-D images. This is what I found." He holds up his holo device and flashes up pictures in color.

"I don't know what I'm looking at." My voice rises with frustration. "Explain what you mean."

"This is the heart." He points. "Here are two legs and two arms, which is good. The head. No horns." He swipes to a new picture, this one clearer, and by the stars, I swear the little creature looks intelligent, and pretty, almost like Danica. But my heart sticks in my throat because the young has delicate green scales up and down its arms. Pointy ears. That's not human or Zandian.

"What?" I shake my head, dizzy for a moment.

"It's a species called Akronicans."

I shake my head. "Haven't heard of them. What are they like?" I flick through images on the screen.

"Well, it's reported that males are extremely violent. Females are nearly non-existent."

"That doesn't make sense. How can that be?" Another image; in this one, the young has its mouth open, yawning. I'm horrified and entranced at the same time. It's like

147

watching a gory battle—I don't like it, but I can't avert my eyes.

"They're reputed to kill their mates after they successfully breed a male young. They kill female young 100 percent of the time. Usually kill the mate if she breeds a female just as a punishment for wasting their time."

"I've never heard of such a thing." I shudder.

The doctor coughs. "When I say *mate*, it's not really a mate. They take slaves and keep them captive for breeding, and kill them after the young is delivered."

I can't comprehend what I'm hearing. "What? Why?"

"It's to do with their genetics." He clears his throat and his voice gains fluency, like he's excited to teach me about this. "When Akronian males breed a male offspring, it doesn't matter what host they use, the resultant DNA will be only Akronian. But if the breeding results in a female young, that one will pick up a significant portion of the DNA from the mother. Their females can use and adopt multiple DNA sources, apparently. Akronicans want to keep their line pure, warlike. They don't want to breed in new characteristics. And they don't bond with mates—they just want male offspring."

"That's repugnant. But Danica, how?"

"Probably conceived the child before you rescued her." His voice is dry. "That's why I thought the fetus was too big at first. She was already pregnant by the time she met you." He answers my next question before I can even ask. "And I guarantee she knew it."

"How can you be sure?"

"She would have been already five lunar cycles along, Gorde. Her menses would have stopped and there are significant changes in a female's body that let them know they are carrying young. I suppose I can't say with 100 percent certainty, but I'm fairly confident she knew."

"And she didn't tell us." I'm confused, and angry. "That she was carrying a young. From a violent, aggressive species!"

The doctor holds up a hand. "We don't—"

I burst out with, "She held it like a sick virus inside her, tricked us into mating her so she could carry the thing here, on Zandia. We told her." I push one fist into my other palm. "We explained how the only beings welcome on this planet are Zandians, and human females."

"She..."

"Completely disregarded it." My anger is so all-encompassing that I can hear the blood roaring in my veins. I grab the device from his hand and scroll through the images. In one, the small creature seems to be smiling, and I don't care for the curve of its jaw—nothing like mine. Or Danica's. "Does it have...*claws?*" I peer at the screen, scowling.

"It appears so, yes. The Akronian males have sharp retractable claws. They usually use them to rip open their mate and, if necessary, the female young after—"

"Stop." Nausea roils in my gut, and I can't tell if it's over Danica's deception, or my disappointment that the young isn't Zandian. "I need to tell Benn. I need—*veck.*" I toss the comms unit onto the nearest surface, the doctor's workstation, and bury my face in my hands. When I look back up, Dr. Daneth is beckoning to Bayla, who comes in, eyes full of concern.

This makes me further enraged—I was tricked by my mate, and stars, now everyone is going to know it. "You can wipe that sympathy away," I snap. "I don't need it, or your pity. Benn and I will deal with—this." I wave my hand at the comms unit, the images. "I assume you already notified King Zander?"

Dr. Daneth shakes his head. "We need to, of course, but I wanted to tell you first. We'll keep this a secret until we determine what to do."

"*Veck*." I look at the comm, as if it has answers.

"Take it." Dr. Daneth clears his throat. "You'll want to show Benn. And Danica."

"Right." I snatch up the unit and stick it into my satchel, hands shaking. "I…"

There's nothing more to say, so I stride out, unable to focus on anything but this revelation, and how my life is falling apart in front of me.

∼

Benn

DANICA'S off visiting our neighbor, Janette, and picking up supplies for her electronics work, and I smile as I glance at the low, long table she uses for her workstation. I'm so proud of her—she's proven to be smart, efficient, and seems to really care about helping Zandia move forward. And now, a young! I start humming the strange tune she sang the other day, and I'm startled when the door bursts open to reveal Gorde, eyes wild, face red with anger.

He holds up a comms unit and waves it. "The young isn't ours."

"What?" I step forward. "You're not making any sense. Who?" But from the sick look on his face, I already know. "That can't be true."

"Dr. Daneth confirmed. The young's nearly full grown and it's Akronian, not Zandian. See for yourself." He tosses me the device, and the pictures, one after another, immediately confirm his words.

"*Veck*. What is this?" I move to a chair and sit, dizzy.

"I *told* you," he snaps. "An Akronian. Apparently a vicious, warlike creature that kills its mates after they bear young. And kills all female young, too. Our *mate*"—and he emphasizes the word with heavy sarcasm—"brought us a mating gift inside her body, Benn. An alien species, a kind which we would kill before allowing on our planet. And she snuck it in. Into our home. Into our lives."

My head swims. "It's a female." I look at the little being. In one picture, an enhanced three dimensional image, it looks almost real, like it's in front of me. I swear it has Danica's smile. But the eyes, the face, the ears— utterly foreign.

A weariness of the likes I've never known settles over my heart. I sink back into the chair, let my head fall back, and close my eyes. "I don't know what to do."

"Maybe we should send her away." Gorde's voice shakes.

My eyes snap open. "Where would we send her?" But I

don't even want to see her right now, so I exactly understand his emotions.

"Jesel, I suppose. I don't *vecking* care where. She deceived us. I couldn't care less where she ends up. But I can't talk to her right now. If I look at her face, all I'll be able to see is that mongrel young."

A clatter from the doorway startles us. We both whip our heads around and there stands Danica, a stricken look on her face, mouth open in a silent *O*.

Her voice shakes. "You know?"

"We do. And I don't understand how you think you would have kept this from us." Gorde stands up and paces, practically steaming.

Danica steps backward. "I didn't—I'm sorry. I didn't know what to do." Her voice is pleading, but also firm. She stands tall and puts both hands on her belly. "And it's not a mongrel. It's mine." Her tone is fierce. "It has nothing to do with Akron, not anymore. It's different. *She's* different."

"But you admit that you did know you were carrying a violent species' young when we met you. Before we mated you."

She nods, slowly. "That's accurate."

"That's deceptive."

"I tried to get away from you." Her voice cracks. "You brought me back. I was going to get on the transport ship, Gorde. But you took me back." She looks up at us, eyes wide, face pale. "You made love to me. Told me you wanted me."

"That was before we knew." Gorde whirls around and punches the wall. "*Veck*."

"If I had stayed with Akron, he would have killed me. And the baby." She coughs. "That's why I escaped, but I was caught by slave traders and put up for auction. Then, you two came along."

"And you used us as your lifeboat." Gorde's voice is bitter.

"I love you." Her voice is pleading. "I didn't expect to, but I did. I do. That has to mean something."

I can't untangle my emotions. "Why didn't you tell us that you were already carrying a young?" I demand, approaching her. As I speak, the full weight of my ire comes out in my tone. "We might have taken you back anyway. Who knows. But now?" I shake my head. "Knowing you tricked us? It's impossible to go on like before."

"I was panicked. I didn't have any other choice." She wipes her eyes. "But you chose me." I hear the abject plea in her voice. "You cared for me."

"No longer," Gorde snaps. "How can I feel the same way after what you did? I can't understand it all all. The utter deception."

"We thought it was our young. We—" I shake my head in disgust. "Everyone thinks it's ours. What in the galaxy do we do now? Tell everyone we have a mutt baby? *Veck*." I bury my face in my hands.

Tears well up in her eyes, and she nods, slowly. "Someday, you two will have a real young of your own." She looks from one of us to the other. "And then you'll understand why I did it. And I hope when that day comes, you can look back on me with sympathy and maybe even forgiveness." Her breath catches in her throat. "I've come to care for both of you and I love you, I truly do. That's why it was so hard to lie to you, this whole time."

"How can you keep saying that you love us?" I roar.

She blinks and flinches. "Because I do. I love you both, and Zandia. I love the friends I've made. I love being able to do real work for the future. I love not being a slave."

"But it was all built on a pretense," Gorde snaps. "*Veck*, Danica, what are we supposed to do?" He sounds as uncertain as he is mad.

"I don't know." Her voice catches on a sob, and she clears her throat. "But I won't allow you to kill my young. I won't." Her voice gains strength. "I'll go to the king, if I have to, and beg for our survival. You can send me away to Jesel or somewhere else, but I will not let you hurt this child. She's smart, Gorde. Benn. She's powerful. She's— she's changed me. And I've changed her." Her voice is wild and fierce. "She's not Akronian anymore, not really. At least not in her heart. I can feel it. I can sense it."

"We wouldn't kill it!" I'm astounded at her words. "Why would you say that?"

"You kill violent species. You told me more than once. You showed me." Her voice is low. She swallows hard. "I needed to give her a chance. To see if she could be okay. I didn't want to lie to you. Mother Earth, it killed me, day after day, to keep this a secret. I wanted to tell you every single second. I know you deserved the truth. Please believe me."

"You're full of lies." Gorde sneers and strides to the door. "How can we trust a single thing you say from now forward?"

"She was the one who helped save us all from Taxx." Her voice rings out and Gorde stops, as if frozen.

"Remember that?" She sniffs and wipes her eye. "Everything happened so fast, and he was going to hurt me, I could tell. He didn't want to, but his hand was so shaky on that gun. And then, I don't know how, but the baby and I—we made him stop. We held him in place so you could take him down."

"That's not possible."

"I didn't think so, either." She swallows hard. "But I can —do things I couldn't before I got pregnant. I'm not the same, anymore. But she's not, either. And she likes you. She already knows you." Her voice and eyes plead with us. "She's not like her father. I swear it."

"I can't handle this right now." The word *father* undoes me entirely, and suddenly I'm at my limit for strange new words and stories. All I want is to get away from this place, this situation, this horrible mess. "I'm leaving, and I don't want to see you when I get back. I don't want to ever see you again."

Gorde roars out a curse. "I don't want to see you again either, or that young. Never in my lifetime. *Vecking* waste of air." He leaves the dome, slamming the door behind him, gets into our transport, and zooms away.

Last time it was Gorde who had to exercise, but today I'm the Zandian who needs to pump my demons out of my body. I take off running, going as fast as I can, in any direction that reveals itself open, until I'm miles away, lungs burning. Trying to outrace my mind, and the images of her in my head.

CHAPTER 14

 anica

I'm in the clinic alone, wondering if I can take the supplies I need and go somewhere in private, and the squeezing feeling comes again. This time I know it's a contraction. My entire belly clenches, and the pain—like nothing I've known before—screams through my nerve endings like liquid fire.

I whimper and sink to the floor, clutching my stomach. My knee twists as I sink down, heavy, and my joints pop and groan, but that's nothing. All I can feel is the knives stabbing me from the inside.

"Guh!" My vision is all dots and static and I vomit, a thin stream of watery liquid that's warm on my chin and breasts.

"Danica? Mother Earth." It's Bayla's voice. I can't see

her, because everything swims in front of me, bursts of red and black and yellow. "What are you doing here?"

"I was looking for—aaaah," is all I can manage. Another contraction seizes me and I fall into it, crying out for mercy, for relief. There's no way I could have done this alone, and I'm glad beyond belief that she's here. "Help me, please."

"I'll get Dr. Daneth," she calls out. "I'll be right back. You're going to be fine."

Her voice does something funny, trailing off into deep low waves of meaningless noise, and I shut my eyes against the flashes of light, as if that might dull the pain.

Time warps, and now the doctor is back with Bayla. I'm on an examination table, and the lights are bright, like the sun, but I'm freezing, shivering, my whole body jerking and twisting from the convulsions.

"Call Gorde and Benn," some being says.

"Lift her up so we can inject the solution into her spine. Now."

Then the pain is magically gone and I'm in a half-slumber, a lovely twilight where all the sounds and colors in the room are magical, gorgeous, relaxing.

Then it's like my dream, that nightmare and I wake up, because my baby is here and she's crying for me, reaching for me, and there's so much blood. They're taking her away, her little face and those pretty little arms with the delicate green scales.

"No!" I scream with all of my might. "No! Don't hurt her! Please, I beg you, just give her a chance. Please!"

Hands hold me back, push me to the table, forcing me

away from her, and as she disappears from my vision, I scream and scream and scream.

I OPEN my eyes and don't know where I am, or what happened. I'm lying in a bed, not my own. White coverings on me. There's a soft beeping sound, and I'm so tired. More fatigued than I've ever been. Suddenly it rushes back and I sit up, wincing at the pain across my entire belly, a dull fire, like some being is pouring salt into a wound.

I gasp and touch my body, only to find bandages. Did they cut me open after all?

"Help," I gasp.

Bayla materializes with a fluid tube. "Sip this," she murmurs, and raises the tube to my mouth.

I push her hand away. "Where's the young. Where is she? Did you hurt her? I need to go get her. I need to get out of here." I try to stand, but even swinging my legs over the bed is an impossible task. I gasp and fall back, panting. "Please, Bayla."

She touches my hand. "Your young is fine, Danica. She's in an incubator because she's having breathing issues, but nobody is going to hurt her."

"But Zandians kill violent species. None are allowed on the planet. I need...to protect her." I'm out of breath and the room spins.

"King Zander said that nobody is to touch her, Danica. Until he's able to talk to you and your mates."

"Nobody will touch her *ever*." I try to sit up again.

"Danica, stop! You're making yourself ill. Please, relax." Bayla gestures to the vitals comm, which flashes up my pulse and blood pressure. Both high.

"I need to see her." It's the only thing I care about right now. Her, and my mates. Except I won't get to see them again, most likely. Such a deception? They won't forgive me. They're probably already talking to King Zander to dissolve our mating. They'll choose someone else. Maybe they'll find their mythical Zandian woman they originally wanted, or a better human. A female who can bear them full Zandian young.

Tears prick my eyes, because it will kill me to see that. Well, if I even get to see it, before I'm sent away.

"Drink the fluids and I'll bring you to see her," Bayla says, so I drink it and toss the container aside.

She puts me into a hover chair and takes me across the room, and there, I lose my heart all over again. Because in the pod, which resembles the med pod on the shuttle, with lights flashing green and red, lies the most beautiful little creature I've ever seen. When I approach, she opens her eyes and smiles, and I start to cry.

"Baby girl," I whisper, and I feel her listening to me, intent on my words. "I love you," I say.

Love you too, comes back, even though I'm not sure I hear her. But I know she feels it.

"Can I touch her?"

Bayla hesitates. "I suppose so? Her vitals are stable, although the levels are different from any other being I've worked with. Her pulse and blood pressure are entirely unique from Zandian/human babies."

She pushes a button and the pneuo lid hisses open.

The baby calmly lifts up her small hands, six perfect fingers on each one, and looks at them. She sticks out her claws, retracts them, then smiles. She pulls the oxygen mask from her face and takes a deep breath. Then she touches her head, brushing away her long silky hair, blonde like mine.

To my utter surprise, she has purple eyes, like a Zandian!

"What?" Dumbfounded, I turn to Bayla, but she's as stunned as I am.

"How can this be?" I reach down to touch my daughter, and at the first contact of my skin to hers, I begin to cry with emotion. I reach down and pick her up, and she nestles into my arms making little happy sounds.

"She's not Zandian. How can she have purple eyes?" I blink at Bayla.

"I don't know. Look she's trying to nurse." Bayla touches the child. "Apparently she no longer needs the supp-ox."

Bayla adjusts my gown and helps the baby latch onto my nipple, where she's soon sucking furiously.

"I didn't tell anyone." I'm filled with guilt and shame. "But I was a sex slave." I shudder with disgust, because being forcibly taken by Akron was nothing like the loving passion I have with my Zandians. *Had.*

"To an Akronian. I escaped because their species kills the female breeder after she gives birth. I had to get away. Give my baby and myself at least a chance." I look down at the being in my arms, feeling overwhelming love for her. "I know no being can understand it, and I apologize for the trouble I've caused by accepting mates here. I know I'll have to leave. We'll leave." The baby mewls, pulling away from my body, at my sudden tension.

"No, Danica. You won't go anywhere." Bayla puts her hand on my arm.

"Are they going to put me into prison?" My heart accelerates. "Just send me away, all right? It will be cheaper and easier, in the long run. I can go to Jesel, where humans are free. I'll take my child and make a life there."

"Danica." Bayla sits down and looks me in the eye. "We understand more than you know." Her voice is full of emotion. "Every human woman on this planet has been in an impossible situation. I'm not judging you. The lives we've led, the places we've been? Well, they lead us to decisions that are all too easy to second guess."

"I'd do it again." My voice is soft but firm. "Even knowing they're going to leave me. I had to do it, for her. She deserves the chance to be more than I am. Than her... father was." I hate calling Akron *father*, but like it or not, he did provide half of her DNA.

At least, to start.

I glance down at my daughter. Oddly, the green scales on her arms are shining purple. "I don't know how this is happening."

A voice at the door rings out. "Danica?" Dr. Daneth strides in. "I may have an answer for you."

He hovers next to my sleepdisk. "Your previous mate was an Akronian. The females of that species are able to mix DNA from multiple sources, even after the embryo has formed. It's unique in the galaxy."

"So when Gorde and Benn and I...ah..." I wave my hand, flushing.

"Yes. The Zandian sperm affected the developing fetus and contributed genetic material to the child."

"So they really are her fathers, too. Both of them?" I breathe out, entranced.

The baby opens her eyes and smiles, grasps my finger with her tight fist.

"I'll have to redo a full genetic mapping, but I believe she is definitely part Zandian now." The doctor's voice is professional but cool. I sense that he's not pleased with this situation.

"Right now you need to rest." Bayla soothes me and strokes my shoulder. "You and the baby, both."

I look to the doorway, alerted by a shuffling sound, but nobody's there. My heart falls.

"Did anyone notify..." I bite my lip.

Bayla looks away. "Just rest," she says softly, patting my hand. "We'll talk more later about what to do next."

Gorde

THERE'S nothing like a mission to distract a warrior from his pain. His heartache. It's better than punching dents into the metal support beams of our dome, which Benn and I have been doing since we found out about Danica's deception.

I can't shake the nausea, the low-grade queasiness that

follows me around. The whispers, *how will you live without her?*

But it doesn't matter. She's not who we thought she was. And if she deceived us about one thing, who's to say she won't do it again?

"Benn and I are going." I don't shout, but my voice holds so much power and conviction that every being in the chamber turns to gawk. "The mission is ours. We took Taxx originally, and we'll bring him back." I clench a fist. "Any arguments?"

Master Seke folds his arms over his massive chest, unimpressed with my bluster.

"Gorde, I think we should disc—"

I cut off my partner. "I didn't think so. Let's go."

I gesture to Taxx, barely restraining myself from ripping his *vecking* head from his neck. Then I remember that I'm just as angry at Danica. And at myself, for trusting her. Falling for her. *Stupid.*

"You'll sit quietly beside me and Benn and you won't lift a finger to touch the craft," I snap at Taxx, as we stride up the steps. "Because you'll be in cuffs. Stealing a craft isn't nearly the same thing as training for many solar cycles to pilot one. Don't do anything stupid, or we will eject you into space and watch you suffocate."

"Understood." His voice is quiet but firm.

"And when we get to the planet, you're going out first, as we discussed."

"Gladly." His voice is stronger now, and holds a hint of excitement.

"You know you're probably going to die, doing this." I don't sugar-coat the words.

"Yes." His answer is simple and quick.

"And yet you're not backing out?" I stop to stare into his face.

He looks back at me, evenly, not flinching. "I'd die for her. For them." He sticks up his chin. "I'm sorry for threatening your mate. I wasn't thinking clearly." He looks away, then meets my gaze again. His mouth twists. "This time I'm doing what's right."

My jaw tightens, but I nod. We board the craft and take our places. Benn cuffs Taxx near the console, and the Zandian sits quietly, although an unmistakable energy radiates from him.

As we speed forward into the inky black, punctuated by far-flung stars, twinkles and dust, I need to ask, "Why didn't you tell us?" It seems to be a common question, lately.

Taxx thinks for a minute, staring out at the universe streaming past us. "They told me that if I alerted you while you came to rescue me, they'd kill all of us. And that if I came back with reinforcements, they'd kill her and the young immediately. But that if I came back with something of value to barter for their lives, they'd consider it. I had to take that chance."

"But you know you'd be walking straight into a trap." I'm frustrated beyond belief. "Let's say you achieved your goal and stole Danica and the craft. Gave them both over. They'd kill you at that point and still sell your human mate and young into slavery. Or hold them ransom." I blow out my breath.

He shrugs. "I had to try. I made the wrong choice. I'm sorry I betrayed Zandia and you. I won't do that again.

There are ways to honor the past and the future at the same time. I wasn't clever enough then, to see it. I'm wiser now."

Benn snorts. "Sitting in prison on Zandia made you into a sage?" He scoffs.

Taxx lifts one shoulder. "I had nothing to do but think." He sighs. "And what I thought was that my mate would be horrified if I hurt another human to help her. She'd want me to do something honorable, even if it meant that I myself was in danger." He swallows. "And so here we are."

"Zandian honor," I muse. "Legend of the galaxies."

Taxx is still gazing out at the stars. "It's one thing that always set us apart. Oh, we have the crystals. Our strength. Skills. But our moral code is well-known. A species who, in the end, does the right thing not just for themselves, but for the good of the galaxy."

My gut twists. Have I been that kind of Zandian lately? But my situation is different. Surely that has nothing to do with honor. It's all about passion, what's right. What's wrong.

Danica was wrong.

Where is she right now? I'm sure she's safe. Bayla notified us that she was at the clinic, and once I knew that, I figured I could ignore her for a while. *Maybe forever.* Thinking of her makes me physically hurt in my chest, an actual piercing pain. I don't need that *vecking* misery.

"We're approaching Hectan-3." Benn's voice is taut. "Masked once again as a bounty hunter. Put on the new facial masks."

The Ocretions were quick to brag about their deep IR

facial recognition technology. *Boastful idiots.* Luckily, we have the human engineer Genevieve and her team, who quickly worked up full face masks that scramble our identities and make us look like Bensai, an even-tempered species who are generally left alone by most species, including the Ocretions.

"This is it," Benn warns, and unsnaps Taxx's cuff. The three of us put on the masks, adjusting them to fit. I'm amazed at how the the two Zandians transform in front of my eyes. If I didn't know better, I'd honestly not know they were my brethren—at least, not until they got closer and I felt the pull of their crystal energy on my own.

"They were being held in the smaller facility in back of the main prison," Taxx says, although he told us this already, during the debrief. I can tell he's nervous from the way he taps his foot, his hands. The quiver in his voice. "So nobody else would know and try to steal them from the captors." He clenches his fists. "I don't know how they're doing." Then he takes a deep breath. "How much time until the Ocretions realize we're not Bensai bounty hunters?"

"No more than a minute after we approach the building, so we'll have to move fast." I open the cabinet and pull out weapons, distributing them to the two Zandians. "Every being know your plan?"

Benn nods. Taxx does too. He's offered to take the martyr's role: He'll go in first; then—if he survives—he'll stay back and ward off any pursuers, only coming back to the craft if it's safe. Part of me is impressed with his dedication. Another part of me still wants to kill him myself.

The stench of Hectan-3 is just as foul as the first time

we were here and my nostrils ache as we take our ground craft near the prison complex. This time we avoid the main gate, and follow Taxx's directions to find the smaller out-building near the cluster of boulders and trash compactors. It's quite far from the main prison, down a faint dusty trail of rocks, almost completely concealed by the abandoned machinery.

"We may be in luck." I halt the craft behind a rusty earth-mover, its bucket locked up, frozen in place like some prehistoric behemoth on top of the cracked red earth.

"They hid it well." Taxx's voice shakes. "Humans and Zandian young are both very lucrative. The guard who has them kept it off the books and didn't want other guards to snag them away from him. They in-fight like vipers, the Ocretions. No trust among thieves."

"Works in our favor." Benn checks his weapon. "Ready?"

We all indicate yes.

Benn looks into my face, then Taxx's. He lifts his arm at the traditional ninety degree angle. "Fight hard, brothers. For Zandia."

"For Zandia," we repeat, raising our arms.

Taxx looks at me for a long moment. "I'll make it right," he says. He turns on his heel and jumps lightly down from the ground craft, graceful and strong, and runs to the silver out-building, weapon raised. He's fast and lithe, and we watch for a moment to see if he takes any shots before we follow.

Everything is silent near us, although we can hear the distant groans and explosions from the mining ops, and random bells from the prison. The only sound is our feet and our breathing, and when we reach the building, we press ourselves to it, on the shadowed side. Nightfall comes quickly on Hectan-3, and it's nearly upon us.

"The door to use is the left one. That's the one they used when they…brought me to visit." Taxx's voice is rough. "It's secured by a level three voice rec but they used overrides all the time. Lazy."

I adjust my stunner to the level needed to destroy the electronic lock. "This'll trip the alarms. Move fast." I blow the door lock, the tiny explosion brilliant, almost blinding, as the metal melts, and the smell of fused steel hits the back of my nose.

"Go-go-go." Benn's voice is urgent, but Taxx is already in, his hand-light illuminating the area, as we rush through the anteroom into a main chamber.

"Mikala!" There's a tone in his voice that slices into my chest, and then the cries of a human woman and two small children fill the room.

Taxx falls onto his knees next to a filthy cot. "Are you all right? Love, are you hurt? I'm here. I've got you. You're going to be all right. I promise it."

"You came for me. For us. You came. Taxx." The human is curled up on the bed, weak, but her eyes glow in the light. "I love you. My love." She reaches up to touch his face, wonder in her eyes. She's like a skeleton: thin, under-nourished.

The two babies huddled near her can't be more than a few solar cycles old—they're terrified; you can see it in their faces, and the way their horns flatten on their heads. When they see Taxx, they smile and scream, launching

169

themselves at him, clinging to him, scrabbling with hands and feet to get close.

The human tries to stand, but can't—I wince, seeing she's injured. There's blood, crusted, old. I don't want to know what they've done to her. At least the young seem unharmed, if terrified.

"We need to go," I snap, as an alarm pierces the air, splitting our eardrums, and lights flash in the near distance.

Taxx pushes the children towards Benn. "Go with him, sons. He'll take care of you. He'll keep you safe."

Benn grabs them up. "Cover me," he growls, and I lift my weapon. "Taxx, grab your mate."

We're nearly at the ground craft when I see them: Three Ocretions, armed with shock sticks and stunners, racing toward us.

"Faster," I shout, and Benn dashes up the steps with the two young Zandians. There's no time to look behind me, but I glance anyway. "Taxx, hurry with Mikala!" I shout. "We have fifteen seconds."

As I speak, Mikala stumbles; in her weakened condition, with her leg mangled, she simply can't move properly.

"Taxx!" She screams, looking at him, just him, the whole time. Her whole body radiating love, concern. "Taxx!"

There's no time—I can see it, we can all see it.

"Take her," Taxx shouts, his voice rough. "Take care of her for me, Gorde. Tell your mate I'm sorry." He raises his weapon and stands between Mikala and the approaching Ocretions.

"Taxx, no!" Mikala's voice is impassioned.

When I scoop her up in my arms, she weighs nothing. A feather.

I race to the craft, panting, and she twists in my arms. "Let me down!" she orders me.

"You can't help him," I snap. "Think of your children."

"I am thinking of them!" Her voice is fierce. "To the left. Look."

It's then that I see it: Another Ocretion darts out from behind a vast, broken down shell of a digger. He's almost at the door of our transport craft when the human in my arms does some kind of twist and is on her feet, waving her arms, getting his attention. "Over here!" she wails, hopping on her one good foot. "It's me you want."

He turns and fires at her, leaving enough time for Benn to shoot him in the head, and when he slides down into the blackness of the ground, she shudders and sways, too, gasping.

I hoist her up to Benn, and look back for Taxx. We can use a longer range weapon and snipe the Ocretions, swing by and grab him as we head back to our main craft.

But his body lies motionless on the ground, and I feel it: He's gone. His mate knows it too, and she collapses into sobs, incoherent, inconsolable, as we fly back to the ship.

Benn

. . .

THIS TRIP IS EERILY similar to the last. This time, though, it's Taxx's two sons in the med pod. Having refused to lie down, wailing for their mother, they are now sitting up with the lid open, holding hands and glancing around them.

I'm no expert, but I figure the crystal energy will help, regardless of their position. At least they're not screaming.

We also have a human. Their mother, Mikala, is weak and ill, and despite the basic medical help we provided, she clearly needs more advanced medical attention. The blast she took from the Ocretion weakened her, and we need to get her back to Dr. Daneth as quickly as possible.

We've given her food and liquids, and used the best med supplies we have on hand, but once she saw that her young were safe, she sank down onto the sleepdisk, rocking and moaning to herself. Crooning the name of her dead mate. *Taxx. Taxx.*

As the adrenaline starts to fade, I get jittery with aftershocks and take several calming breaths. "Why can't she settle down?" I gesture at Mikala.

Gorde grunts. "She's overwhelmed. Human emotions."

"Should we give her a sedative?"

"Dr. Daneth said no. I talked to him over the comms. He said if possible, if she doesn't go ballistic, to wait until we land."

I nod, but I'm feeling emotional, too. I had no great love for Taxx, but the way he sacrificed himself for his children and his mate, to give them a chance at life on Zandia? That was noble, and regardless of his past actions, I admire him for it.

I walk over and crouch down near Mikala on the sleeping platform. "You're safe here," I tell her, again.

She doesn't respond, but at least she stops chanting. Her bare toes clench and curl.

"I'm sorry about your mate. Taxx—" I take a breath. "He died saving your life and your children. That's a good legacy."

She looks up now, and although her face is dirty and crusted, I can see her beauty. Not like Danica, but pretty in her own way. "It's not fair." Her voice wobbles. "He did everything right."

I look away. *Not everything.* "He did his best. You'll remember that about him, and teach your children. They'll be safe on Zandia, and so will you."

She nods, but her eyes are bleak.

"Nobody will hurt you there."

"But my children." She gestures. "They're not—they won't have a father. Will they still be welcome?"

"Of course." I respond automatically. "All Zandians are welcome, and desired. Human females, too. Because..." Then I hesitate. It would be thoughtless to talk about another mate for her, when she just lost Taxx.

"Because we are compatible mates." She looks down at her feet. "Taxx told me." Her voice cracks and her small hand clenches on her dirty garment. "But what being would want a human mate who already has young from another male? I can never change that."

Without thinking, I take her hand, not with passion, but with compassion. "There are all kinds of families, Mikala. You may find the perfect mate who wants you and your young." I squeeze her hand. "Because they like you just as you are. Without changes."

Then I suck in my breath as a thought occurs to me.

She tilts her head, questioning. Even in the midst of her despair, she—like other humans, *like my human*—is quite perceptive.

I shake my head. "Why don't you wash up, put on clean clothing? Eat? I can show you." I make my voice coaxing and soft. "If you take care of yourself, you can take better care of your young. Right?"

She nods, finally. "Thank you. Yes."

As she moves to take care of her own needs, and her young, I sit for a moment, lost in thought. Wondering what the *veck* I'm doing with my own life.

Danica

"THE KING WILL SEE YOU NOW." Bayla smiles at me and touches my arm. "Don't be worried," she adds in an undertone. "Everything will be fine."

No, it won't. I don't say it out loud because Bayla's too sweet and I don't want to disturb her. Everything is far from fine.

The young squirms in my arms. *Calm, Mama.*

"It's okay," I whisper, dropping a kiss on her soft forehead. She chortles and blinks her amethyst eyes—so like both her fathers'.

That thought gives me a pang in my chest, so painful I

have to stop walking for a moment. I suck in a breath and push forward. The sooner I get this over with, the better. The anxiety of not knowing my future is killing me.

As I walk into the palace's Great Hall to meet with the king, I hold my baby tightly and curtsy, dropping my eyes. "My lord."

"Danica." His voice doesn't sound angry or aggressive. "You are well?"

I bounce the baby, even though she's not fussy. "I'm feeling fine." Nursing the baby gave me unexpected energy, and my wound seems to have healed ridiculously quickly. "Thank you for seeing me, my lord. It's important I speak with you."

He raises a finger and a hoverchair is placed in front of his throne by one of the elderly servants. "You may sit."

His eyes are not on me, though—they're glued to my young, examining her. I hold her a little more tightly. My nerves are on high alert. If he tries to take this young from me... Well, I don't know what I'll do. But it won't be pretty.

"Dr. Daneth said she was born green. Now she's purple." He leans in closer. "She has purple eyes, too. By the stars." He trails off and blinks. "It's incredible."

I swallow and nod. "She is. Yes." My voice sounds choked.

"He said she has hardly any Akronain DNA left, and the gene segment for violence is entirely missing."

"I could tell." I'm eager to explain. "I knew it, my lord. She told me that she was good and nice. She asked me to keep her safe."

"Yet you didn't tell any being."

"How could I? Who would believe such a thing? I barely understood it myself." I cuddle her in my arms. "But as time went on, I believed she was going to be kind and gentle. I just needed her to have a chance. I was scared to say the truth, because…"

He meets my eyes with a shrewd regard. "Because you served an Akronian master. One of the most violent, feared, unstable species in the entire galaxy."

"I escaped to save my life and that of my unborn child."

"You didn't tell my warriors you were already with young when they accepted you as a mate."

"I did not."

He waits, so I continue. "I'm sorry for the deception, but at the time, it seemed like my best chance for survival. And hers." I nod at my child. "It will always hurt my heart that I deceived them and you, but I will not lie. I'd do it all over again if the situation were the same."

I stand. "I understand if you wish to send me away. I request that I be delivered to Jesel or another neutral territory. Please don't sell me and my young as slaves." I shudder, a cold trail runs down my spine.

He frowns. "Your mates have forsaken you?"

I bow my head. "Yes, my lord. I don't think they will forgive me."

He regards me for a long moment. "They may not," he agrees, and it seems that there is some compassion in his face. "You will need to ask them."

"I cannot." I look down at my child. "They were not present for her birth. They do not wish to see me. They said as much."

The king stands from his great throne and paces away.

"They are on a rescue mission, Danica. They didn't know you were birthing the young."

"Oh." Relief for a second, then my despair returns. "Even if they did know, our last words—they were not kind ones." A tear comes to my eyes. "So, is it Jesel, then?"

One time, it was all I wanted. Now, the idea of leaving Zandia tears me in pieces. But it's my only option.

"Is that your desire?" He turns to look at me.

Surprise that he's asking what I desire spikes. It's definitely not what I desire, but it's the only option I see. Why would I stay on Zandia if Benn and Gorde didn't want me?

"I'll arrange a transport ship for you both, then, as soon as you're cleared by Dr. Daneth for travel."

"Dr. Daneth said I'm clear," I lie. Because I can't stand to stay here one more planet rotation.

King Zander's eyes narrow, like he knows I'm lying, but before I can bluster out more story, something flashes in my mind. A sound.

I put a hand to my head, and grimace.

"Danica?" The king steps closer, concern on his face. He waves a hand and one of the servants rushes forward to scoot the hoverchair beneath me.

"No." I shake my head, adjusting my baby with the other hand. She squirms, and suddenly she's focusing along with me, the two of us. Listening. With her at my side, the noise is amplified and all at once I know what it is.

"Gorde and Benn. Their ship? It's in trouble. I can hear it." I suck in my breath.

"Danica, they're still in the Ramban territory," he says

with a frown. "They won't be back for hours yet. There's no way you could hear anything. And," he adds, "last check in, they were fine."

Bayla enters and he gestures her over. "Danica may be having some post-partum issues," he says in an undertone. "Please, help her get back to the med bay for a check up and have Dr. Daneth notify me when she's cleared for travel."

"You need to listen to me." I raise my voice. "I sometimes hear things. Things I couldn't before. I think it's the effect of her." I nod at my child. She gurgles as if agreeing with me.

King Zander lifts his brows. "Precognition? Like my queen?"

"No," I snap, impatient.

"Danica." Bayla's voice is calm. "You're having a hallucination. We can help."

"It's not a dream," I stand. "I hear it. There's something approaching them. You need to tell them." I wince and squeeze my eyes shut as the sound happens again. "It's a war ship, arming missiles."

"How do you even know that sound?" Bayla's voice is doubtful, but the king watches me thoughtfully.

I blink. "My old master enjoyed playing gory holos." My voice is taut. "To terrify me. He'd tell me that if I didn't get pregnant soon, he'd set me adrift in a dummy pod and tell the nearby ships that I was a free test target. Would play me all the fighter craft sounds and ask me which one I'd like to be the last sound I'd ever hear in this life. Make me recite them back to him by name if I wanted to avoid a beating. Trust me, I know the noise."

"Danica…"

"It's an S-class battler with long-range destroyX missiles," I hurry to add. "Older, but quite effective. And cloaked. Favored by undercover Ocretion pirates."

King Zander frowns but raises an eyebrow. "That is, indeed, their preferred craft."

"Look, just communicate with them," I beg. "If I'm wrong, no harm done. It will take just a second to check. But if I'm right…" I trail off. They may not be my mates anymore, but I couldn't stand the thought of them dying. "One call. I'll go back to the med bay and I won't bother you again."

He hesitates, then turns to the guard beside him. "Make the call."

CHAPTER 15

 orde

"What are you thinking about?" I turn to Benn, pretty sure I already know, from the expression on his face.

"Danica." He sighs. We're silent for a minute, and the only sound is the faint thrum of our engine as we speed towards Zandia on our rescue craft.

I glance over; the rescued human and her two young are fast asleep in the sleeping platform in the far alcove, a silvery flight blanket draped over them, but I lower my voice anyway. "Specifically?"

"When I was talking to her"—he gestures to the human female—"Mikala, I realized we were too harsh with Danica. At least, I was too harsh."

I don't reply. He continues, "I told Mikala there are all

kinds of families in this galaxy." A tendon twitches in his neck. "Maybe...we were too hasty to push Danica away. Perhaps the three of us could work, anyway."

"You're saying you could accept another creature's young?" My voice rises, even though I've been thinking the same thing.

"Maybe." He tilts his head.

"You didn't even want a human, to start," I scoff. "Now you're willing to add an Akronian to the mix?" But I think back to the pictures on that comms unit. That small face, the green arms, the smile. Danica's smile. Something tightens in my chest. "Although I suppose it's not really completely Akronian at this point. Right? It has her, too."

He nods. "It does. I mean, it didn't look...completely unpleasant."

"No," I'm quick to agree. "It was actually somewhat acceptable. For being green. And scaly."

"There was that one picture where it sort of had its mouth open, the way Danica does when she sleeps." He laughs.

"The one where its eyes were shut. Yes. That did look like Danica." I smile, remembering how Danica sometimes snores—very lightly—and gets incredibly upset when we tease her about it.

"And if anyone talked? I'd shut them up." He raises his fists and growls.

I nod. "If we accepted her and the young, the others surely would too."

"Why would it be a big issue?" He shrugs. "After all, it's only one being out of many. Isn't Zandia known for our honor, like we said? What's more honorable than giving another little being a chance?"

I smile, then it fades. "But she deceived us. And we have no idea what this creature will be like, in its personality." My shoulders tense.

"If it's at all like her, it will be delightful. And we can shape it as it grows, to honor Zandia and everyone here. And we could have more young." Benn's voice is light. "There's no reason we can't have a whole swarm of Zandians, if she's still fertile."

"True." I glance over at Mikala again. Remember how she put herself in harm's way to save her children without even a second thought. Like it was instinctive. Like breathing. That's clearly how Danica feels about her young already. "Humans love their young with a strong power. And if Danica loves the next ones as much as she loves the first…"

He nods. "Exactly. That's the kind of mother we need for Zandian young."

I summon up her image in my mind. "She'll probably deliver it soon. *Her.* The female young." I remember Danica's fear when we first talked to Dr. Daneth. "Do you think they'll need to…cut her open? To take her out?" It makes me cold inside—in a way I've never felt in battle. Not even back on Hectan-3, fighting the Ocretions. I shudder.

"I don't know." Benn's voice is uncertain. "Dr. Daneth said that the Akronians use their claws to rip apart their mate to dispose of them. Perhaps she had thoughts about that?"

"*Veck*." I feel sick with guilt. "And we left her alone. We need to get back there to support her. No matter what happens, we must be by her side when she needs us."

"If she even still wants us. We left her alone and said awful things to her." Benn's voice is rough. "Maybe she'd prefer different mates, ones who are more considerate."

"She's not having other mates!" I shout, then lower my voice when Mikala stirs and moans in her sleep. "There's no way. We're getting her back, Benn. I swear it."

"If we can." He turns to the console. "What's that?"

"Incoming call from Zandia. Emergency frequency." I grab the unit. "Gorde, Benn, go ahead."

"Check your perimeter." Master Seke's voice rings out into the area on speaker. "Ensure your masking is functional. Check for tails."

"On it."

Benn and I snap into action.

"Nothing," Benn reports, tension in his voice. "I did a 360 and there's nothing within fifty l-segs. We're clear."

"Check again." Seke's voice is insistent. "Use the newly installed surveillance technology."

When our commander orders, we obey, but I wrinkle my brow as my fingers fly across the console. "What am I looking for?"

"An S-class battler with long-range destroyX missiles. Possibly cloaked with new tech and laser. As good as ours."

Benn pulls up the galaxy map and our ship blinks, a sole dot in a sea of black. "Still nothing."

Seke sighs. "Good. I'm glad to hear it."

"What intel did you have?"

"Your mate claimed she could hear it."

"What?" Startled, I frown and raise my voice. "How?"

"It's complicated. I'll debrief when you return."

I lean forward to glance at the screen. There's something there, a ghostlike flash, just for a second. "Benn, what's that?" I point.

His voice rises. "Stars, it's a ship. It's an Ocretion battler. In attack position."

"This is neutral airspace."

"When do the Ocretion pirates care about that?" He grabs the control deck. "They're ready to fire. Going into z-speed to avert. Hang tight."

Our ship lurches forward, and the AirPulse locks us into place as the relentless g-forces tug our bodies. Across the ship, Mikala and her young awaken and cry out, screams of fright, but there's no time to console them. We just need to get away from this enemy ship— it's ploddingly slow compared to our fightership, and once we're a safe distance away, there's no way they can catch up.

"*Veck!*" I sink my arms onto my knees, heart pounding, sweat breaking out onto my forehead. "That was close."

"What's happening?" Mikala calls out, one young in each arm. "Are we in danger?"

"We were. Not anymore." Benn goes over and sits on the edge of her sleeping platform. "Ocretion pirates tried to sneak up on us, but we saw them and space-jumped. They can't catch up, or find our location now."

"Thank Mother Earth." Her eyes flutter and she leans back. "I just want to be safe."

Danica's words. For some reason, I feel her presence

so strongly that I almost think she's here. I close my eyes for a second and see her face.

We've lost one Zandian today. We nearly lost a human and two Zandian children.

I've had enough losses.

We have to win Danica back.

CHAPTER 16

"Where is she?" I stride up to Master Seke, the male who trained Gorde and I from a young age to be warriors. Now that Mikala and her young have been taken to medical support, I need to find my mate.

"Slow down." He holds up his hand and frowns. "We need to discuss this."

"I need to see her. We both do." I gesture at Gorde, who's right on my heels.

Gorde adds, "We want to be there for the birth of the young. We need to see her."

Seke shakes his head. "She delivered the young last planet rotation. King Zander has her slated for transport to Jesel."

"What?" I shout, panic engulfing me. A spike of cold fear pierces me. Our vulnerable mate—sweet Danica—has been banished? It's all our fault. Gorde and I, as her Zandian sponsors, abandoned her. Right when she needed us most. Now she's gone through childbirth alone and is being sent away with a tiny infant and no being to protect her?

Gorde is a thundercloud beside me. "Why?" he booms.

Master Seke holds up a palm. "I understand she requested the deportation, herself."

Gorde and I go still. Ice cold washes over me.

Oh Zandian star, how could we let this happen? We hurt her so badly she wants to leave. She's running from us. Again.

A punch of illness hits me when I realize how alone Danica must be. How afraid. And it's no wonder she wants to leave. She just had an Akronian young. I told Danica we kill intruders. She probably promised to leave to prevent any harm from coming to her young.

"Where is she?" Gorde asks at the same time I say, "We must see King Zander. She cannot be sent away."

At that moment, King Zander enters the dock. "Benn, Gorde, a word?" He points to the space in front of him and we rush over to stand at attention before our ruler.

"You've forsaken your mate?"

"No!" we both shout.

"Forgive us, my lord. Yes, we did, but it was a mistake. We wish to remain mated. We will sponsor Danica. Please don't send her or the young away."

King Zander considers us. He's hard to read in the best of moments. In this one, I have no idea what he's thinking. Finally, he says, "I will allow her and the young to remain on Zandia." I heave a sigh. I know he has the capacity to do difficult, hard things for the good of Zandia. This could have gone the other way, if he thought it necessary.

A huge wave of gratitude rolls over me. "Thank you, my lord." I bow, relief making my voice shake.

"The young must be observed for any signs of violence. Her asylum here is provisional."

We both bow. "Thank you, my lord."

"Go get your mate. She is in the med bay."

And as we stride out the door, I think I hear him mutter, "Every time, with the human mates. Every time it's something."

CHAPTER 17

MY DAUGHTER IS restless for her fathers. I sense her thinking of them, because I get little flashes she sends to me of their voices. Each time, a sharp pang twists in my heart. How will I ever tell her that she can't have them, know them…and it's my fault?

I soothe her by nursing and soon she falls asleep, a little curl of golden hair falling across her soft, pale purple face. Her long lashes flutter on her cheeks, and with her claws retracted, her tiny fingers are so sweet and perfect, although right now she has them fisted up by her head. She smells like fresh grass. I kiss her head. *Mine.*

A rustle at the door has me looking up from my cot, and I gasp, because there they are: my mates. Benn. Gorde. Wearing their mission gear, stinking of sweat and adrenaline, faces lined with worry—and I've never found them more handsome.

I stand, leaving the young covered with a soft blanket and step forward, my whole body intent on them. "You're safe!" Tears come to my eyes, as relief and joy surge.

"Of course we are." Gorde strides forward and takes my hands in his, touches my face. "And you are, too. Thank the stars." He acts to pull me to him, then hesitates. "You're—please, sit down. You must need rest." His jaw stains a deeper purple and his mouth twists. "We weren't here for you." His hands linger on me, running over my forearms, stroking. Like he can't stop touching me. "I'm sorry."

Benn comes forward too. "It was you who told King Zander to warn us." He touches my hair, winds it into his fingers. There's wonder in his voice. "You heard the pirate ship coming."

I nod, look at the baby, back at him "Yes." I sit down on the edge of the sleepdisk and touch her back, softly, as she sleeps. "Well, both of us." I look at her soft blonde hair covering her little face.

"You saved us from an attack." Gorde's voice is low and gravelly. "Our ship is strong, and we could have fought and won. But you prevented us from taking damage. Amazing."

"I was connected to you." I offer a wobbly smile. But my stomach flips.

"You're safe? You're healthy?" Gorde sits beside me, takes my hand in his. As always, I marvel at how strong and large his fingers are compared to my small ones. I always felt protected, having him hold my hands. But now I'm full of anxiety.

Are they here to say goodbye?

"I am. They had to cut her out." I lift my tunic to show the incision. "But like Dr. Daneth said, I'll recover." I act like this is no big deal. In fact it's not: so many things have happened since then. It was a million sun cycles ago already.

Benn's face blanches and he sinks into the chair beside my sleepdisk. "Did it hurt? Are you in pain?"

"No physical pain, not right now." I shake my head.

"And the young?" He swallows. "She's healthy, too?"

"Yes. She is. I need to tell you—"

"Wait. Let me go first." He stands back up, comes closer. He puts his hand onto my cheek and cups it, gently. "Gorde and I, we talked. Danica, you can't go to Jesel. We won't allow it. You belong to us. We're sorry we had our heads shoved up our asses, but we need you. We want you back. Even if the young isn't ours." He swallows. "There are all kinds of families in this galaxy, all kinds of ways to make a home. Maybe she's not a Zandian. But she's part of you, and that makes her precious."

Gorde squeezes my hand. "Danica, we're still not happy about the deception. But we understand why you did it. You must have been terrified."

I nod through my tears, which suddenly blur my vision.

Gorde continues. "We can have more young, Zandian young. This one will be"—he pauses and laces his fingers into mine—"their sister. She will be like you, and because of that, we will treasure her. Do you understand?"

I sob out a half-laugh. "You mean it? You really want me back?"

"Do you want us back?" Benn's voice is uncertain.

"A few moments ago I thought I was going to Jesel." I wipe my eyes. "But my whole heart is here, with you. Come closer." I tug at Benn's hand, and he sits beside me, on the other side, so I'm sandwiched between my two mates. "Of course I do. I've never stopped loving you."

"Then we are still together." Gorde's voice rings out loudly, and the young stirs. I twist back and reach between my mates, who shift to allow me access. I stroke her back and murmur, but she whimpers and rubs her little fists over her eyes, turning.

"She's waking up." My heart pounds. They don't know, yet. What will they say when they find out? "Do you want to see her?" I pull back the cover and shift her so Benn and Gorde can see her face, her limbs. Even dressed in the one-piece soft cloth outfit, her purple skin is clearly evident.

The two of them lean in, entranced.

"But she's not green." Benn's voice halts. "She looked green, on the console pictures. Danica?" He turns to me abruptly.

"She has purple eyes!" Gorde shouts it out, a grin spreading across his face. "They were wrong, Benn. All wrong. She is Zandian!"

"She's complicated." I put a hand on his arm to calm him. "She started out Akronian and human. But along the way...when you two mated me, she incorporated your DNA as well. And changed herself."

"But that's impossible." Gorde reached out a finger to her horns, pulls back. Extends it again. "Can I touch her?"

I laugh. "Of course you can. You're her father." I flush and lower my voice, feeling a surge of new emotion. "Both of you are. She's unique in the galaxy now. There's nobody like her, ever, anywhere."

"Unique like Zandia." Gorde puts both hands under her little body, then pulls back. "Ah, I don't know how. Show me?" He flushes purple. "This is new to me."

"To me, too. To all of us." I smile at my two mates. "Like this, see? You have to support her head with one hand. Scoop with the other." I lift and place the baby in Gorde's arms.

The sight of my strong, fierce warrior holding a tiny girl makes my heart sing. "You're a natural."

"I want a turn, too." Benn runs one finger down her cheek. "She's such a light purple color."

At the touch, the baby opens her eyes. I feel her surprise and joy when she sees Benn and Gorde. *Here! Mine!*

"Yes, yours," I agree, squeezing her little foot softly. "Your fathers are here now."

"Is she talking to you?" Gorde's eyebrows go up.

I flush. "She communicates with me without talking. She already knows you two from your voices. She missed you."

Gorde transfers the baby to Benn's arms, and they both bend over, staring into her face. Smiling at her. Talking to her, saying their names. When each of them touch her small cheek, I almost choke up.

"So we need to talk about these, ah, powers you seem to have." Gorde raises one eyebrow, a few minutes later.

"It started when I became pregnant." I stroke her little toes. "I could hear things, even really far away. And I can communicate with her. Sometimes, I can make things move." I think back to the cuffs. "Or hold them in place." Taxx. "Not all the time, and I can't direct it. I don't know; if I practice, I might get better. But I was trying to pretend it didn't exist."

"I knew there was something else going on." Gorde's voice is triumphant. "Something you weren't telling us."

"I'm sorry." I look up at him. "It was too strange. No way to explain it, and it was confusing to me."

"It's in the past." He looks down at the child, then to me.

"Well, not really. It's still here, now." I smile and touch his face.

"I know." He laughs. "What I mean, is that the secrets are in the past. Yes?" He looks down at me.

"Yes." I smile, relieved. "Definitely."

Benn strokes my thigh, holding the baby with one hand. Already comfortable with her. "What's her name?"

I pause. "I didn't pick one yet. I was waiting, just in case you two…" I trail off.

Gorde clears his throat. "There's an ancient Zandian word, *marea*. It meant *future*."

I try it out. "Marea. That's lovely."

Benn squeezes my leg. "I like it too. Marea."

The baby waves her tiny fists. Then she squeals out a little peal of laughter.

"I think she agrees." I touch her chin. "Do you like your new name, Marea?"

Happy. Sleep. Marea closes her eyes in Benn's arms.

"Well, I guess it's decided." I laugh.

Gorde takes my hand. "Good." Then he leans in and whispers into my ear. "And once you're properly healed, little human, Benn and I are going to have to punish you for all of these secrets, my love." The look on his face makes it clear that the punishment is going to be of the enjoyable variety.

"Oh, you will?" I lean in and rest my head on his strong chest.

"King Zander typically remands disobedient humans to their mates for correction," Benn agrees. "And I think we may need several thorough sessions to make sure you're properly disciplined." He runs a hand lightly over my thigh, the touch at once a caress and a tease.

"Maybe each night?" I suggest hopefully, looking from one strong Zandian to the other. "And in the morning as well, just to make sure I remember?"

"Definitely." Gorde growls and bites my neck. "As often as we can manage it."

CHAPTER 18

G orde

OUR DAUGHTER IS SLEEPING. I check to see that her eyes are shut, and they are, her purple lashes brushing her pale lavender cheeks. She makes a little snorting noise as she slumbers and I smile, pulling the covers over her shoulders.

I grab the YoungWatch holo monitor, enable Sound-proof, and close the door. Then I head back out to the common area, focused on Danica.

"I think it's time for a reckoning." I raise my eyebrows and cross my arms. "Dr. Daneth gave us the go-ahead, my love."

"So he did." Danica steps out of the alcove.

I catch my breath. "*Veck*, beautiful, what are you wearing?" I stride across the room. "I can see your pussy through it." My cock hardens instantly at the sight of her in those tiny panties.

"You like it?" She preens and sticks out her hip, putting her hand there. "Gossamer lace. It's new. Benn, do you think it's nice, too?" She runs her hands over her breasts. Her nipples are already hard.

Benn groans. "Danica, you know I do."

"Why don't you come show me how much," she teases, pinching her nipples. "I'd rather have your hands on me than my own."

"Gladly," I growl, taking her into my arms and sticking my tongue into her mouth. She returns the kiss, eager, her hands exploring my chest, my abs, and winds one long leg around mine, pulling my hips closer to hers. The kiss goes on as Benn comes up behind her and gets to his knees.

"Spread your legs," he urges her. "Don't stop what you're doing. I'm going to lick you while you kiss him."

"Mmmm." She makes a little noise into my mouth and puts her leg down, widens her stance, all the while kissing me. I feel her body shake as he slides the panties down her thighs. I know the instant his tongue touches her because she moans again and clenches up before relaxing.

"Shhh, enjoy it," I murmur, reaching between us to finger her nipple. "Let us both bring you pleasure."

"Mmmph." she nods, then surrenders to my mouth.

I tease her with my tongue, and play both nipples with my fingers, tweaking, rolling, pinching them. Soon enough, with both of us working her body, she starts to make little moans of arousal, and her kisses become more urgent. When I move to bite her neck, she cries out and lets her head fall back, panting a little.

"Are you close?" I wind both hands into her hair and palm her head. "You want to come?"

"Yes," she whispers, eyes shut.

"Then it's probably time to punish you," suggests Benn, letting go of her thighs and leaning back on his heels. He wipes his mouth with one hand. "You're delicious, baby, but we still need to chastise you for lying to us, you know."

"That's right." I reach back and give her a light slap on the ass. "King Zander said to make it a good one. Really teach you a lesson."

"Mmm. And we always obey orders from our ruler," Benn agrees, getting up. "In fact, we even acquired a new implement just for you."

"What?" Danica's eyes fly open, half alarmed, half aroused.

"Oh, you'll find out soon enough." I pull her back for a kiss. "I don't think it will be your favorite, though."

"You're so bad," she complains, but when I reach down to cup her mound, she sighs in pleasure. "Yes, there," she whispers.

"Not yet." I scoop her up in my arms. "Benn, where shall we do this?"

"Let's bend her over the ottoman." He points. "With her delectable, bare ass pointing upward for the leather strap."

Danica squeaks. "Leather strap?"

"It will probably hurt a lot," Benn promises her. "Definitely remind you never to lie to us again." His voice is serious.

She sucks in a breath. "Benn?" She looks from him to me. "Gorde?"

I put her down. "Don't you agree that you need to put this behind us?" I raise an eyebrow.

She bites her lip. "Yeees, but—"

"Then do what we ask, love." I flick one nipple.

She makes a mewling noise. "Should I be scared?" Her face is a little wary, even aroused.

"Probably." I smile. "Lie down on your stomach, legs as wide as you can spread them." I gesture to the ottoman. "Don't worry about reaching back; we'll tie your hands."

She reaches down tentatively to touch the ottoman, looks at us again, then lies down. Spreads those *vecking* creamy, perfect thighs. She's so wet that her pussy glistens in the light, and she pushes her hips down into the surface of the ottoman, seeking relief.

"No," Benn warns her, as he comes over with a silky cloth. "Not until later, love. Put your wrists together."

When she's tied up, the red of the cloth gorgeous against her pale skin, we both stand over her, admiring her lush form. Spread out for us like a *vecking* feast.

She shifts and moans. "What are you going to do?"

I fetch the new strap from a storage bin.

"Hmm," I say, running a finger over the thick, shiny surface. "It's a little stiff, being so new. But your ass will help it soften right up, I'm sure."

She clenches her buttocks and new moisture appears at the juncture of her thighs.

"Oh, you just think you're going to like it." Benn runs

his hands over her body. "But I promise it will sting like the devil, Danica. And we won't stop until we think you're really sorry."

"I already am sorry," she whispers, shifting her thighs.

"Not as much as you will be." He slaps her ass once, and my cock twitches as a red mark blooms on the soft skin.

"Ouch." She bucks her hips.

Benn slaps her again, and again. "This is what happens to naughty humans who lie to their masters. They get a hard spanking that turns their ass cherry red."

"Mmmmph!" she mutters, twisting her hands in the cloth. "Ow."

"My turn." I'm going to die if I don't get a chance to touch and spank my mate.

Benn moves aside and I kneel down beside her. "You ready for more?"

I spank her hard, not waiting for a reply, again and again, right on her sit spots. "Going to go harder now, baby, to really warm you up for that strap." I raise my hand high and crack her across both buttocks, gratified to hear her cry out. Loving the way she twists to get away from the punishing blows. The way she gets even wetter when she can't escape.

"You ready to apologize?" I rain a flurry of spanks right at the base of her thighs, and she thrusts her hips up at me.

"I'm so sorry." She gives a little sob, and I check her face—she's still enjoying this, rough as it is. But she's crying.

I wipe away a tear. "What are you sorry for?"

"That I lied. That I had to lie. That the universe can give us impossible choices, sometimes."

"Aw, baby, that's cheating." Benn chuckles as he comes in front of her, cups her chin in his hand. "This is about you, not how the galaxy tosses dice."

I stroke her ass, soothing the burn we've surely ignited. "We only want an apology for your part, Danica."

"I really am sorry." She turns her head, looks at me with those gorgeous blue eyes. "You know it's true."

I wipe another tear. "Just to be sure, though, how about a dose of the strap? Benn?" I slap my thigh, enjoying the way her body jumps at the sound, and hold out my hand. "How many should we give her?"

"Start with ten and go from there," he suggests. "That should be enough to make her sore tomorrow, but not so much that she can't enjoy her regular routine."

"We'll reserve the strap for serious punishments." I run it over her ass, and she quivers at the touch. "When she really needs to be chastised. When we bring out the strap, she'll know she's really in trouble."

"That's right, Danica." Benn strokes her hair. "If you come home and see the strap lying on the sleepdisk, you'll know that you're in for a serious punishment later on."

"Maybe we'll even send you a comm picture of it, a close up." I turn the strap sideways and run it slowly between her legs, making sure that it presses down into the crack of her ass. I push, and she sucks in a breath. "So you can think about it all day, and know what's going to happen later."

"No," she murmurs, but when I move the strap, I can see how *vecking* wet she is now. She's practically dripping.

"You don't get to say *no* to us." I stick two fingers into her, unable to resist. She makes a sound of satisfaction, and I groan, her warm moist body calling to me.

"Taste this, baby." I put my fingers to her mouth. "Suck your juices from my hand. This is how turned on you get when we talk about punishing you. You like being mastered by us. You thrive on it."

"The pain and pleasure both." Benn smiles. "She *vecking* loves it."

"And she knows she needs this."

She shifts and whimpers and I can't wait a second longer.

"I'll do the first five," I decide. "You'll finish it."

I stand up and adjust the ottoman so it floats higher, giving me the perfect distance to swing the strap at her ass. "I think she's ready. Ass up, love. Push it higher. I really want to see you reach for this punishment."

I wait until she pushes up her hips, raising her ass to me. Then I lift the strap and bring it down, hard, right across both cheeks.

There's a loud crack, a second delay, and then she howls.

"Ouch!" She twists furiously, but Benn grabs her tied hands and whispers into her ear. "That was just the first one, Danica. Nine more to go. You earned it, so you force yourself to take it."

She sobs and nods, stills her body.

"Ask me to continue." My hand itches. I don't know if it's right or wrong, but *veck*, I love having her tied down at my mercy, taking my stripes. I want it to hurt. Then I'll make it better.

"Pl...please, Master Gorde, continue whipping me."

The sound of her voice saying the word *whipping* inflames me. I raise the strap and slap it down again, this time at the base of her cheeks, and she screeches as the red stripe appears. "Ouch," she whispers, closing her thighs, pressing one foot into the other.

"Legs open." I tap her thigh. "And they stay open, unless you want a few strikes of the strap here?" I stroke her pussy.

She squeaks in alarm. "No, Master Gorde, not there."

"That would certainly not feel good later, when we *veck* her," Benn observes. "She'd be smart to keep those legs open."

She likes it when we talk about her—we've discovered it gets her hot. She likes the element of danger even more.

"I'll keep them open," she promises, sliding her legs wide again, showing us that delectable cunt.

"See that you do." I surprise her with a swipe of the strap, then another, so fast that she can't cry out in between. I give her the last of my five, a good hard one, while she's still processing the first two, then I toss the strap to Benn. Coming around to the front of the ottoman, I take her face in both hands and kiss her, passionately, and she responds instantly, her mouth opening to mine, her tongue greedy.

"Just a taste," I whisper, "of what you'll get if you take the last five without complaining."

"But if you ask us to stop, or say a single word"—Benn stands beside her and lays the strap across her buttocks— "we'll *veck* your ass and pussy but not let you come until much later this evening."

"Oh, please," she whines, shifting on the surface.

"No *please* about it. Just obey." Benn teases her with the handle of the strap. "Feel this? You like this in your pussy? Take your strapping and you'll get nice, hard Zandian cock instead."

"I'll be good," she breathes, her voice barely audible.

Danica

I'M TIED down and my ass is on fire. This hurts almost as much as the cane, and I still have five to go, but I'm turned on beyond belief. I think I've never been this wet in my life!

"Gorde will keep you company up there while I finish the conversation with your ass. But first..." Benn chuckles, then pushes the handle of the strap deep into my pussy a second time. With my legs spread so wide, I can't quite clench down like my body is dying to do, but I squeeze my muscles, unable to resist.

"Oh!" It feels so good, and I need more.

"Oh, indeed." He pulls it back out and in, out and in. Fucking me. "Ride it, Danica. Show us how much you want our cocks." He shoves it in harder.

I'm shameless, and I do as he bids, pushing my hips as hard as I can to reach the handle, which he moves, tantalizingly out of reach, making me work for each contact. "Please."

"Surely you can do better." He tsks at me. "Do I have to

give you an extra with the strap as motivation?" I hear the hiss of the leather flying through the air, and then the pain explodes on my ass, mixing with my pleasure in a way that's indescribable.

"Fuck!" I scream, bucking my hips, and he slides the handle back into me for a second.

"This? This is what you want?" He runs it over my clit, and it's so wet by now from my juices that it slides easily over my skin.

"Mother Earth," I gasp.

"Or did you want this?"

He removes the strap and strikes me again, even harder than before, right across both ass cheeks, and I wail. It *is* what I want. I want it again, harder, more. I cry out my need, wordless sounds, sobs of desire.

"Smell your sex in the air. The room is full of your scent. Your desire." He straps me again. Again. Again.

The pain and pleasure are mingled inextricably and I'm flying now, lost in a sea of sensation. I'm so wet and needy that I can't think straight.

I hear the strap fall to the floor and it takes me a second to realize that they're done punishing me. Benn picks me up and tosses me on the hoverseat. "Hands and knees," he orders, his voice taut. "I'm going to *veck* you good and hard, Danica, and come in your tight pussy."

I'm barely in position when his huge cock presses against my entrance. I'm so wet that he slides in without any issue at all, and when he starts pumping me, I sob in pleasure. This. This is what I need. What I want.

"Missed this so hard," he mutters, pumping me. In.

Out. Balls deep. "Gonna let you come, baby, even though you don't deserve it," he whispers, and that inflames me so much that I can't hold back.

The orgasm explodes, sending me into a bliss I've never known, pulses of white-hot lightning, over and over. "Benn," I cry out, as the feeling keeps coming.

"Danica," he roars, and bites me hard on the shoulder. His cock tightens and I feel his essence flow into me, hot.

"I THINK IT'S MY TURN." Gorde grabs me as I come out of the shower. "I've waited long enough."

I giggle and squeak as he tosses me down onto the hoverseat. Across the room, Benn lounges, naked, on a hoverchair. Smiling.

"Your turn for what?" I tease. "Cooking me dinner? Cleaning the..."

My words turn to a sigh as he buries his head between my thighs and finds my clit with his tongue. "Ahhhh."

He looks up at me for a second, his eyes glowing with passion. "My turn to pleasure you," he says simply, then puts his head back and sends me into the stratosphere.

I reach down and grab his horns, stroking them with my fingers, feeling them harden under my touch. At the same time, my clit throbs with desire as he licks me, flicking his tongue in a way that drives me mad. When he sucks my clit into my mouth, I almost levitate.

"Gorde!" I cry out.

He smiles down into my face. "I love you."

"Me too." I melt at the sight of his strong, fierce jaw, his gleaming eyes. Full of passion, for me. "I love you too."

Still looking at me, he nudges my thighs a little wider. "Open for me, baby. Let me in."

"Always." I wiggle and tilt my hips, and he presses down, and our bodies find the perfect angle so he can slide in. "Oh, Mother Earth. So good."

I shut my eyes and hum as he pushes in deep. He has this way of twisting as he comes out, and he hits all of my spots. He can usually make me come so fast.

"Wait for it, baby," he urges, and I open my eyes to see his expression. That small smile on his sexy lips. Those chiseled Zandian jawbones.

He stops moving and just waits inside of me, and I swear I can feel his pulse in his cock, and my heart matches it. I reach up to touch his face, amazed at how close we are. How much I care for him, for Benn. For all of us.

My ass stings in a delicious way and my whole body is in tune with his. As he moves again, I grab his arms, his shoulders, pull his body to me while he fucks me. And when we come at the same time, I cry out his name, with a rush of pleasure and joy so immense that I know that life could never be better, not on any planet, not with any other beings.

My story is a strange one, my path unusual. But it's led me here, to Zandia. To a love greater than any I've known. And I know, without a doubt, that the future is going to be amazing and bright.

***

Thank you for reading *Bought by the Zandians*! If you enjoyed it, we would really appreciate it if you would leave a review. Your reviews are invaluable to indie authors in marketing books.

WANT MORE? MASTERED BY THE ZANDIANS

Mastered by the Zandians
Zandian Brides, Book 3

Mirelle

"Hurry, hurry," I whisper, my voice hoarse with urgency. "Faster." I nudge the taller female with my hand. "Come on."

Her wide eyes, glazed with anxiety and stress, are uncomprehending.

"Do you speak Ocretian?" I swipe sweat from my brow and cough. It's the most common language in the galaxy, and these are human slaves--surely they understand my words. "If you want to leave, we do it now."

The smaller one lurches into motion. "Mama, come on!" she wails, and tugs at her mother's hand. "Please." Then she coughs; the air here is inhospitable for human lungs. But the woman stands frozen and starts to tremble.

Fuck.

I've rescued over fifty humans, and this isn't anything new, but it's awful timing. Because out of the corner of my eye, I spy a being across the galactic ship lot look over with more than a passing glance. I've been noticed.

I don't need any being watching me, figuring out who I am and what I do. It's dangerous enough to even be here on this planet. I shouldn't have come, but I can't resist humans in need.

I assess him the way I was taught, scanning quickly: Muscles. Horns. Purple skin. Daggers at the waist. He's a Zandian, a small but powerful species of warriors who recently took back their planet. Double fuck--he's the one who outbid me at the auction.

"My ship is just 800 paces away." I take the woman's hand. "What's your name? I'm Mirelle." The Zandian is eyeing us. Even across the tarmac, which sends up heat ripples, I see his amethyst eyes flashing in the brutal sunlight.

She blinks at me and I curse. "Mother Earth. You come with me, it's safe passage to Jesel, where humans are free. You wait around here? They'll take you back to that auction, punish you for leaving, and sell you off to a sadistic monster." I'm not sure that's true: The Zandian, who won her purchase, surely plans to take her to his planet. Zandia. But there she'll still be a slave. I'm offering her something far better.

The woman finally moves, jerking her neck. "I don't know what to do. Help me."

I scoop up the smaller girl, even though it's probably the mother who needs assistance, but this spurs her into action--she follows me as I jog to the ship. But just as I set down the child and unlock the portal, allowing the entrance steps to descent, I see motion.

It's the Zandian. Mother Earth, although I know I need to get out of here, watching him move is like magic. He's fast and graceful, like a wild animal on the plains. Intent.

My two rescues suddenly feel the urgency because they scamper onto my well-worn craft, but it's too late for me to follow, because he's here. In front of me. Backing me up against my own ship. The one I constructed with my own hands back on Jesel from old parts scavenged from galactic trash.

He looks right at me with those purple eyes. His horns are alert. "You have property that is rightfully mine."

I don't speak. I assess him, watching as he leans forward, his quad muscles tensing. Ready to attack,

215

although his arms are loose. And I sense his adrenaline in the air, his odor. Masculine. Powerful. He must assume I'm weak, because I'm so small. Fool.

"I am from Zandia," he continues. "And you have absconded with two females that I bought. Turn them over or I will take them from you."

I take a slow breath in. Out. Transfer weight to the balls of my feet. But I don't say a word. I've learned silence is an advantage; it confuses opponents. Plus, my voice would give me away. I dress like a male and play my role flawlessly, but it's hard to disguise myself when I speak.

His eyes shift to the entry of my craft, and I make my move. I dart forward and jump, twisting in the air as I do, my left metal-toed boot connecting hard with his jaw.

He groans, I think from surprise and anger more than pain. Still in my aerial twist, I whip around and land, crouching low, then shoot out my leg and wrap it round his, going into the tumble I practiced for a year straight back on Jesel. The move is automatic, all the bruises and breaks merely preparing me for this. Life or death struggle against stronger opponents.

When I tug my leg forward, he topples, as expected. But what I didn't anticipate was for him to catch his balance so quickly! While I'm still on the ground, he somehow manages to right himself and grab at me.

"Surrender," he commands, his strong hands pressing into my shoulders, pushing me down into the baked ground. It burns through my camo gear. I kick out auto-matically, but he straddles me, one strong thigh on either side of my lean torso. His body heat affects me just as intently as the radiated sun on my back.

I pant and look up into his eyes, letting him see mine are green--that always confuses an opponent. I'll know when to move. One second. Two. Mother Earth, his eyes are so clear, so intelligent. The curve of his lip--is he smiling? How cocky. I'll show him who's in charge.

I swallow and watch his eyes dart to my lips, my neck. His smile fades; his expression turns to one of consideration. Like he's trying to figure something out.

That's it. I harness all of my energy into my buttocks and legs, then twist and turn.

He grunts and shouts but I'm away from his hands, those powerful hands.

Back on my feet, I crouch, bounce, staring at him.

He's up too, and as we lock eyes, I feel a tension I've never experienced. When he was over me, his face already victorious, I can't describe ---

He lunges, his fist raised.

I block him, child's play, then use another aerial leap-- a new one.

But fuck, it's like he anticipated it, because he blocks my kick and then he's got me again, and he's pressing me up against the hot metal hull of my craft. Arm against my neck, other hand grabbing my arm. Hips pressed into my body. Thigh to thigh.

His breath is hot on my neck and smells--oddly-- sweet. Not fetid, as I might have expected for a warrior. I ignore the tingling feeling in my skin from his proximity.

We're both panting.

"Who are you?" he demands. "Answer me."

I stare at him, defiant. He's not going to get a word

from me. My headgear has come loose in the struggle and my red hair spills over my shoulders.

"*Veck*, you're a female." His voice is full of disbelief. "And you're human?"

And he figured that out, too. I supposed it wasn't too hard.

"How did you learn to fight like that?" He sounds grudgingly impressed. "And why are you trying to steal my slaves?"

I grunt and shake my head. I've never had such trouble getting away from an opponent. Zandians are clearly just as good as the rumors say.

He eases harder into my neck, an easy push, and gives me a smirk. Showing me he's in charge now. Pressing his advantage. And despite the pressure on my windpipe, and his unyielding body holding me back, tingles flit across my skin again. In my neck. My belly. My nipples. What in Mother Earth?

I suck in air, forcing myself not to panic. Then I shift my hips and he immediately matches my move with his body, pressing himself to me even more closely. His hand moves on mine, but he doesn't release me. This Zandian has no intention of letting me go.

"I'm taking back the other females," he says, his gaze direct. The air from his lips, from his words, as he speaks, blows on mine. "And you know what? You're coming with me." He grins at me, and in that moment--for reasons I completely don't understand--I almost want to melt into him. To reach up and touch those chiseled jawbones. Those lips. Those oddly enticing horns. His skin.

His body is lean and hard, muscles everywhere. His

lips hover only inches from mine, and for a split second I think he wants to lean in and kiss me. I've never done this, but I've seen others--

I need to take every advantage. I dart my tongue out and lick my lips, and make a small, breathy murmur. The kind of thing I know females do when they want to entice a male. At the same time, I press my hips forward and whisper something to him that he can't understand, because it's in English. A dead language. Words I've only recently learned.

"My name is Mirelle, and I'm a freedom fighter."

I sense his surprise and interest, and once again, I use the opportunity. Elbow drop, then up. Arm press and push. Knee up. Battle scream right into his ear, high and piercing, the first loud sound I've made.

And I'm free, once again, and he's on the ground, a stunned expression on his face.

And that gives me the few seconds I need to leap into my craft, shut the door, and blast off this godforsaken ugly planet with my precious cargo.

My craft is slow but steady, and I know that if I just get enough of a head-start, nobody can find me.

But worry pricks at my neck: The Zandians, it's known, have upgraded ships. The fastest in the galaxy. Cloaked. With every advantage. If he follows me...I don't know what's going to happen.

No way am I letting anyone take me hostage. Because this is my life's work--helping rescue humans, bringing them to safety. And no being is going to stop me, unless they kill me first.

Mastered by the Zandians

I can fly a fighter jet in my sleep and kill with the fingers of one hand. I work alone.

No being in the galaxy can challenge me -- until I tangle with two strong, purple Zandian warriors. And crash my ship.

They say I stole their cargo, and they plan to take me to their planet. Make me theirs.

Nobody owns me. I'm not going to let these Zandians master me, no matter how sexy and appealing they are.

Because I have a secret mission. And if they find it out, my entire life could be over.

My name is Mirelle, and this is my story.

WANT FREE BOOKS?

OTHER TITLES BY RENEE ROSE

Sci-Fi

Zandian Masters Series

His Human Slave

His Human Prisoner

Training His Human

His Human Rebel

His Human Vessel

His Mate and Master

Zandian Pet

Their Zandian Mate

His Human Possession

Zandian Brides

Night of the Zandians

Bought by the Zandians

Mastered by the Zandians

Zandian Lights

Kept by the Zandian

Claimed by the Zandian

Stolen by the Zandian

Rescued by the Zandian

Other Sci-Fi

Alpha Mountain

Hero

Rebel

Warrior

Daddy Rules Series

Fire Daddy

Hollywood Daddy

Stepbrother Daddy

Master Me Series

Her Royal Master

Her Russian Master

Her Marine Master

Yes, Doctor

Double Doms Series

Theirs to Punish

Theirs to Protect

Holiday Feel-Good

Scoring with Santa

Saved

Other Contemporary

Black Light: Valentine Roulette

Black Light: Roulette Redux

Black Light: Celebrity Roulette

Black Light: Roulette War

Black Light: Roulette Rematch

Punishing Portia (written as Darling Adams)

The Professor's Girl

Safe in his Arms

Paranormal

Bad Boy Alphas Series

Alpha's Temptation

Alpha's Danger

Alpha's Prize

Alpha's Challenge

Alpha's Obsession

Alpha's Desire

Alpha's War

Alpha's Mission

Alpha's Bane

Alpha's Secret

Alpha's Prey

Alpha's Sun

Shifter Ops

Alpha's Moon

Alpha's Vow

Alpha's Revenge

Alpha's Fire

Alpha's Rescue

Alpha's Command

Midnight Doms

Alpha's Blood

His Captive Mortal

All Souls Night

Alpha Doms Series

The Alpha's Hunger

The Alpha's Promise

The Alpha's Punishment

The Alpha's Protection (Dirty Daddies)

Wolf Ranch Series

Rough

Wild

Feral

Savage

Fierce

Ruthless

Two Marks Series

Untamed

Tempted

Desired

Enticed

Wolf Ridge High Series

Alpha Bully

Alpha Knight

Step Alpha

Midnight Doms

Alpha's Blood

His Captive Mortal

Alpha Doms Series

The Alpha's Hunger

The Alpha's Promise

The Alpha's Punishment

Other Paranormal

The Winter Storm: An Ever After Chronicle

ALSO BY REBEL WEST / ALEXIS ALVAREZ

Read More by Rebel West / Alexis Alvarez

Zandian Brides Series (with co-writer Renee Rose)

Night of the Zandians

Bought by the Zandians

Mastered by the Zandians

Zandian Lights

Kept by the Zandian

Claimed by the Zandian

Stolen by the Zandian

Sci-Fi Romance

Conquered by the Alien Prince: Luminar Masters, Book 1

Steamy, Contemporary Romance

Perfect Match

A Handful of Fire

Boston

Dream Girl

Kinky/BDSM Romance

His Firm Direction

Casey's Choice

Capturing Kate

Myka and the Millionaire
Return

ABOUT RENEE ROSE

USA TODAY BESTSELLING AUTHOR RENEE ROSE loves a dominant, dirty-talking alpha hero! She's sold over a half million copies of steamy romance with varying levels of kink. Her books have been featured in USA Today's *Happily Ever After* and *Popsugar*. Named Eroticon USA's Next Top Erotic Author in 2013, she has also won *Spunky and Sassy's* Favorite Sci-Fi and Anthology author, and *The Romance Reviews* Best Historical Romance. She's hit the *USA Today* list seven times with her Wolf Ranch books and various anthologies.

Please follow her on:
   Bookbub | Goodreads | Instagram

Renee loves to connect with readers!
www.reneeroseromance.com
reneeroseauthor@gmail.com

ABOUT REBEL WEST

Rebel West writes hot sci-fi with aliens so sexy you'll swoon! She's into photography and travel, and when she's not figuring out ways to get her main characters together, she's out with her camera looking for inspiration. Find her under her other pen name, Alexis Alvarez, where she writes contemporary romance and kinky/spanky/BDSM books.

Read More by Rebel West / Alexis Alvarez

Sci-Fi Romance
   Conquered by the Alien Prince: Luminar Masters, Book 1

Steamy, Contemporary Romance:
   Perfect Match
   A Handful of Fire
   Boston
   Dream Girl

Kinky/BDSM Romance:

Hammered

His Firm Direction

Casey's Choice

Capturing Kate

Myka and the Millionaire

Return

Her Vampire Temptation

Newsletter: https://goo.gl/forms/iVRhZbk2s0mz8v6h2

Website: http://graffitifiction.com/

Amazon Author Page: https://www.amazon.com/Alexis-Alvarez/e/B0107LJQEM

Facebook Author Page: https://www.facebook.com/AlexisAlvarezAuthor/

Goodreads: https://www.goodreads.com/author/show/14127116.Alexis_Alvarez

Twitter: https://twitter.com/AlexisAlvarezWr

Instagram: https://www.instagram.com/alexis_alvarez_writer/

EXCERPT FROM CONQUERED BY THE ALIEN PRINCE

BY REBEL WEST

"What you deserve," he snaps, his eyes wicked, "is a hard spanking right now for your continued insubordination. You take that, and maybe I'll consider rewarding you."

He's hard under my body, and I know that this time he won't be able to stop, no matter how many meetings he has.

"Do it," I whisper into his ear, and bite the lobe, hard.

He growls and presses his hands against my body. "You don't know what you're asking."

"Yes, I do. I want it."

"You really do?" He pulls back to look into my eyes.

I stick up my chin. "Are you afraid of me?"

He laughs, a dark, dirty chuckle. "Far from it, Cali. But once I start, you might be the one who experiences a little frisson of fear. You think you can handle that?"

"Yeah. I do." My voice is tough, confident.

He smiles, and suddenly my stomach flips. I'm prey, and he's the hunter. And I fucking love it. He scoops me up and puts me on my feet, in front of him. "Let's see you ask for it, then. Last time you disobeyed me, do you remember what I threatened?" He raises an eyebrow and touches his belt.

My whole body sparks, like I touched a live wire. "You told me... you'd use the punishment strap on me, if you needed to spank me again." My nipples are hard with desire.

"And here we are," he says conversationally. "And I do need to spank you again. So unfortunately for you," he slaps his thigh meaningfully, raising one eyebrow, "and your tender ass, this punishment is going to be far more memorable than the last one."

He unbelts something from around his waist. It looks like leather, and it's a lustrous black. Supple. My breath catches in my throat with fear and desire. The mixture is a drug to my veins.

He doubles it up and slaps it into his palm. "But we'll start with my hand, like last time. Come."

He nods at me and points to the spot between his spread legs.

I swallow hard and walk back to him, stand in between his thighs, feel the warmth of his body.

"Remove your garment, like last time." His voice is granite, and I wonder if it's taking all his willpower to play with me like this first, instead of just toss me onto the bed and fuck me hard.

Fumbling, I undo my jeans and slide them down my legs, and then off. I hold the denim in my hands until he takes it from me and tosses it behind him on the bed.

"This time we'll start without the panties," he says softly. "Give them to me, please." He holds out one hand.

When I hesitate, he snaps and points at my crotch, and I flush hard, then slide the panties down and step out of them. These he tucks into a pocket in his pants, and the sight of this is erotic enough to make my nipples harden and a surge of moisture flow between my thighs.

"Assume the position, Cali," he says, patting his lap. "We'll start this way at least, to warm you up for the strap. And as a reminder, you are to call me Master while I am disciplining you."

I slide over his lap, sucking in a breath as his strong, warm hands grab and reposition me.

"Thighs as wide as you can, please."

"Yes, Master." I do it, barely able to handle the suspense. My whole body is aching for his touch, rough, soft, all of it. I want it all.

"Good." I sense him raising his hand.

"Hold on!" I grab his leg. "Just a minute. Please."

"What?" He stills his movements.

"I'm—will it hurt more than last time?" I gulp, unsure about the strap.

"It will." He lays one hand on my buttocks and rubs. "Still no more than you can handle, but it will be worse than last time. You will tolerate it, even if you don't like it." He bends down to whisper, "After all, don't you deserve to be punished for your transgressions?"

Why does this shoot flares of arousal through my body?

"Yes," I answer, my skin on fire. "I do."

"Relax your buttocks. You know my rules." He taps my ass.

I force myself to soften my muscles.

"Your bottom is so soft," he remarks, stroking my skin. "It will be a pleasure to punish you and turn it red." Without warning, he lands a hard slap across my left ass cheek.

"Ouch." Before the word is fully out, he spanks me again on the other ass cheek, and begins a firm, punishing rhythm. He spanks harder than he started last time, and before long I am kicking up my feet and twisting on his lap.

"Stop moving," he warns, directing a volley of spanks at my sit spots, "or I'll do this." The spanks increase in intensity and then he slaps the base of my thighs until I cry out, "I'm sorry! I'll stop."

"See that you do," he tells me, and returns to the original pattern of spanking all over my ass.

It's hard not to wriggle and squirm, because my ass is already burning beyond belief, and the sting is making me want him so badly I could almost come right across his thighs, lying here, without even a touch to my clit. "Are you almost done?" I whimper.

He pushes my thighs apart and slaps his hand right onto my pussy. "I'll tell you when I'm done. Don't ask again. Your job is to take what I give. If you ask again, I'll spank here." He slaps again, harder, against my soft nether lips, and I almost fly apart.

"Lock," I beg. "Master," and I don't know what I'm asking: *Stop, more, please?*

"Shush," he commands. "Lie still and accept your punishment. We still have quite a ways to go."

Conquered by the Alien Prince by Rebel West
    <u>Amazon and KU</u>

CONQUERED BY THE ALIEN PRINCE - SAMPLE

Conquered by the Alien Prince
Luminar Masters, Book 1
An Alien Sci-Fi Romance
By Rebel West

A sexy silver alien with ripped abs, a top-secret patient with a mystery illness, and unicorns – and Dr. Emily Taylor's experience on Luminar is just getting started!

It's not easy being one of Earth's top neuroscientists at age twenty-four, but Emily's dedicated her life to research, leaving little time for dating. When she travels on a confidential mission to Luminar, her local delegation lead – handsome Prince Lock, turns out to be domineering in all the right ways to bring out her passion.

But he's an alien prince and she's an earth human, and there's no way they could have a *real* relationship. Plus, anti-human protestors and threats against the Luminar monarchy are causing havoc, putting her mission, and maybe even her life, into jeopardy.

This interplanetary romance will need to have a bond of steel, because the glorious nights of kinky passion are just the start to an everlasting HEA.

Enjoy the first book in the Luminar Masters Series by Rebel West. The books are interconnected and can be read in any order. Guaranteed HEA and no cheating!

Note: This book contains elements of dominance and submission. If this material offends you, please do not buy this book.

www.ingramcontent.com/pod-product-compliance
Lightning Source LLC
Chambersburg PA
CBHW020720130726
47899CB00011B/588